SPECIAL MESSAGE TO READERS

THE ULVERSCROFT FOUNDATION
(registered UK charity number 264873)
was established in 1972 to provide funds for
research, diagnosis and treatment of eye diseases.
Examples of major projects funded by
the Ulverscroft Foundation are:-

- The Children's Eye Unit at Moorfields Eye Hospital, London
- The Ulverscroft Children's Eye Unit at Great Ormond Street Hospital for Sick Children
- Funding research into eye diseases and treatment at the Department of Ophthalmology, University of Leicester
- The Ulverscroft Vision Research Group, Institute of Child Health
- Twin operating theatres at the Western Ophthalmic Hospital, London
- The Chair of Ophthalmology at the Royal Australian College of Ophthalmologists

You can help further the work of the Foundation
by making a donation or leaving a legacy.
Every contribution is gratefully received. If you
would like to help support the Foundation or
require further information, please contact:

THE ULVERSCROFT FOUNDATION
The Green, Bradgate Road, Anstey
Leicester LE7 7FU, England
Tel: (0116) 236 4325
website: www.foundation.ulverscroft.com

NEMESIS

A burlesque beauty's fierce yearning for vengeance is triggered following the callous shooting of her younger sister in a gang war. Rita's single-handed efforts to avenge her sister's death bring her into contact with some of gangland's most ruthless killers, whose animal instincts cause them to treat life cheaply, and women callously. Through many dangers Rita pursues her determined way towards the clearing of the mystery surrounding her sister's slaying, and the vengeance which has set her whole being aflame . . .

Books by Norman Firth
in the Linford Mystery Library:

NORMAN FIRTH

NEMESIS

Complete and Unabridged

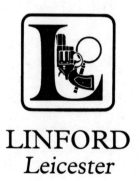

LINFORD
Leicester

First published in Great Britain

First Linford Edition
published 2015

A catalogue record for this book is available
from the British Library.

ISBN 978–1–4448–2591–6

Published by
F. A. Thorpe (Publishing)
Anstey, Leicestershire

Set by Words & Graphics Ltd.
Anstey, Leicestershire
Printed and bound in Great Britain by
T. J. International Ltd., Padstow, Cornwall

This book is printed on acid-free paper

1

'Sandy,' growled Al Inman, editor-in-chief of the *Morning Sphere*, 'you'd better hot-foot it over to the island and get a line on this shootin'. Horne was just on the 'phone and he figures it's another of those gang shootin's. But this time there's some dame involved. Grab Simpson on your way out and try an' get some pictures.'

'Sandy' Dale Farnes grinned cheerlessly, and answered with a drawl:

'Okay, Al. Though why I have to be around whenever some routine job like this throws up, I'm darned if I know. I was reckonin' on coverin' that suicide over on Valderbilt. There's a society chick named Phyllis Mauveen over there; seems she got tired of bein' a playboy's doll and threw herself out of the window at Lassal's Hotel. Eighteenth floor. I bet she's a sight.'

'She'll keep,' snapped Inman. 'The

morgue's open day an' night. This other business is more urgent. We've followed these shootin's for the past three weeks an' I guess there's something big behind 'em. It's about time we got a line on what's brewin' in the mob world. It's my notion some big-shot's horned in from out of town and is tryin' to take over from Cornell. If that's so, it's likely we'll see both outfits wipin' themselves out, an' that oughta make good front-page stuff. It's about time somethin' turned up to scotch Cornell's set-up once and for all. The cops ain't gettin' anywhere. Too much graft, I figure. So go see what's what. If this new shootin' links up with the killin' of Lynx Larsen last night, you can concentrate on the story — because it's obvious someone's out to reduce Cornell's outfit numerically.'

'What makes Horne pin this on that theory?' Sandy demanded. 'Has he identified someone in the car?'

'Sure! One of the guys is young Pete Beamish — one of Cornell's smoothies who operated the Kitkat Club over on Tenth Avenue. There'll be plenty of

2

trouble over this, you can bet your pay-packet. Cornell won't sit down and take this kind of thing philosophically. He'll probably tear the town apart until he finds out who's behind it.'

Sandy nodded, thoughtfully. Inman hollered: 'Well, don't stand around like a tintyped stupe — get out. Let's have something for the public to get hysterical about. Get some pictures. Find out who the dame is . . . let's have some good background stuff on young Beamish . . . '

Sandy nodded. 'I'm practically there,' he told Inman. And, swiveling around, he strode through the door and made his way down to the garage.

Kelly, the mechanic, was putting the finishing touches to some work on the engine. Sandy greeted him and commanded:

'Okay, Kelly. I gotta go. Is she runnin' right now?'

'She's sweet enough now,' he was told. 'Sackful of grit in the pump, but I got it out.'

'You're the best nurse a jalopy ever had,' enthused Sandy Farnes.

'And you're the screwiest news-peddler this organization ever hired,' returned Kelly. 'We've had a few nuts on this paper in my time — and I've been here eighteen years. But you're the nuttiest of the lot. Maybe that's why I'm so fond of you, Sandy. And since I'm fond of you, here's a note of caution for your book. Don't stick your nose into Cornell's business too deep. I knew Cornell when he was a school-kid back in Thornville. That guy was never finished off when the Creator made 'im — he's got neither heart nor conscience. He'd kill as casually as anyone else'd strike a match.'

'Thanks for the tip-off,' Sandy said, somberly. 'But you forget, I've been around. I'm not exactly a tenderfoot. It's my job to stick my nose into trouble and get the inside dope for the sufferin' public. Kinda a crusade, y'see, Kelly?'

'Then keep your rod well-oiled, son,' returned Kelly, shaking his tousled old head sadly. 'An' buy yourself a third eye. For the back of your neck.'

Sandy laughed, slid into the jalopy's driving-seat and maneuvered the long, freshly-polished coupé out onto the street.

He put his foot down as soon as he reached the highway, and sped over the bridge, heading for Hope Island, the small promontory joined to the mainland by the new suspension construction.

Lieutenant Marty Horne looked up with a grimace as Sandy Farnes walked over to the group of cops and homicide experts clustered around the stationary jalopy. The car — a big green sedan — was parked by the side of the road: a long, lonely stretch of highway straggling through the low, dusty plateau.

'You must've heard there was a dame mixed up in this,' Horne grunted, staring intently at the reporter.

Sandy chuckled. 'Inman gave me the assignment,' he announced. 'Seems it was your own tip-off. What's goin' on here anyway?'

'Looks like a gang shootin',' returned Horne, bluntly. 'Nasty business. Pete Beamish is one of the stiffs. There's a dame with him. The other guy ain't been identified positively, but we've got a

5

notion he's one of Cornell's triggermen. Big brute with a face like a shoved-in gorilla.'

'A fine description,' murmured Sandy. 'Could fit a thousand guys. Might even describe you.'

'Yeah?' returned Horne, dryly. 'Well, never mind the backchat, Carrots. And where's our picture brigade? I'd have expected you to roll up with a gross of cameramen and a walkie-talkie outfit.'

'I figured you'd veto the idea of us taking snaps,' said Farnes, cheerfully. 'Time enough to play watch-the-birdie when I've thought up an angle for rousting the police department over their incompetence.'

'Just as well.' Horne grinned. 'You don't get any pictures this trip. Our own boys are havin' attacks of nausea over this set-up. But come and take a look for yourself. We were just gonna transfer the stiffs to the wagon.'

Farnes walked across with the police lieutenant to the scene of the tragedy. It was not a pleasant sight. Inside the car were three bodies: two on the front seat

— a man and a woman — and one slumped over sideways in the back.

Pete Beamish had been driving. His body was lolling over the wheel, hands still resting over the ivory circle. Blood smothered the front seat, and it was evident that none of the victims had died very quickly. On the other hand, there were so many shots distributed among the unfortunate corpses that Farnes was completely stupefied and dumb. He looked curiously as the surgeon completed his final examination of the girl. Her chest, neck and arms were riddled with bullet holes, and blood completely soaked her bodice. It was impossible to see exactly what she looked like, but she was a young girl, maybe around twenty or so, with quite a good shape.

The smudge-and-dab boys were still floating around, but it seemed to Farnes that they were trying to set light to a flame: surely there was no sense in looking for fingerprints? Whoever had done the job had, seemingly, used a machine gun or a quick-firing automatic — or maybe there had been two or three gunmen on the job.

'Okay now, Doc?' asked Horne.

'Done all I can do here,' replied the doctor. 'I'll finish off at the morgue.'

'Good enough,' said Horne, somberly. 'Okay, boys. Take 'em out and load the casualty wagon. Have the immediate area searched for any signs of a scuffle or any weapons that might have been dropped. Although it looks to me as though this bunch was ambushed by some other jalopy and the shootin' pretty quickly carried out. Guess they were taken by surprise — there seems to have been no attempt to get out of the sedan, or to make a fight of it. Yet all these birds were totin' irons — even the dame had a jewelled pistol in her purse.'

Some of the plainclothes and uniformed cops hurried around making themselves useful. The interns from the ambulance treated their cargo with the disdain and casual indifference of morons; the sight fairly sickened Sandy, who was used to that sort of thing himself, but who saw a whole heap of horror in the sight of three bullet-drilled corpses being loaded into the wagon.

Horne said: 'I gotta find out who the dame is, and who that guy is in the back. If he's one of Cornell's boys, we ain't heard the last of this business by a long shot.'

'Yeah, reckon Cornell will be good and burned up over this,' commented Farnes.

'Burned up is just what that guy *will* be one of these days,' returned Horne grimly. 'If ever a guy was labelled for the hot-seat from birth, it's Woolf Cornell. The swine's as slippery as a well-greased eel. But we'll get him,' he added confidently.

Farnes nodded. He didn't doubt that the cops would get Cornell in the long run: or, if he did have any doubts, they were simply fostered by the thought that some other mob would catch up with the gangster first. And, on the face of things, there was already some opposition to Cornell's operations, on the boards. The night before, Lynx Larsen, Cornell's best gunhand, had been shot dead in a speakeasy uptown. Now — Beamish and some other guy.

Where the girl figured in the deal was a mystery. Nothing was known of a girl answering the description of the corpse with Beamish. The only molls known to the cops and the newshounds were the usual flash and lusty babes who hung around the Kitkat Club and other joints operated by Cornell as legitimate covers for his more spurious and nefarious deeds. There was nothing in the grim calendar of crime to which Cornell wouldn't stoop, and the cops already had their eye on his mob for sundry killings, snatches and successfully-run rackets. The trouble was nailing down definite evidence to convict. There were so many loose-tongued mouthpieces available to spring the mobsters that holding onto them once they were pulled in was like trying to nail down a packing case with safety pins.

The cops had plenty of information, boatloads of suspicion, but no proof. And evidence had to be backed by concrete proof.

As for the molls, the cops never bothered too much about those. The gangsters had to have some feminine presence to keep them happy, and the police department figured that the usual women who haunted the precincts of Cornell's joints were simply near-prostitutes who had a perverted idea about the value of a gangster as a protector. It was their business, and as long as they stayed on the right side of the law, the cops had other troubles to keep them awake nights. The advent of the girl in the Beamish sedan, however, was something different. It was the first time any woman had been mixed up in gang trouble. And the girl in question was not, superficially, one of the over-painted, pseudo-tough hussies usually found hobnobbing with the wide boys. She was dark and neat and more like a city typist than a gunman's mistress.

Farnes agreed with Horne's opinion on that score, and as they separated to enter their own vehicles for the ride back to town, Farnes figured his best plan for the moment was to stick close to Horne's tail and find out a little more about the girl.

Beamish, too, was column-copy. The *Sphere* could afford to devote a couple of columns to Pete Beamish. He was a 'name', a celebrity around town. Tall, dark, immaculate and debonair (in life), Beamish had puzzled lots of people who knew of his close connections with the gangster Cornell. Although Beamish was outwardly nothing more than the real 'king' of the Kitkat Club, there was more to it than that.

Something more than mere morbid curiosity took Farnes to the morgue that evening: Horne had stressed his determination to identify the dead woman, and concentrate on her killing more than upon the shooting of Beamish and the other guy. As Horne saw it, the deaths of the two men were directly attributable to the fact that they were Cornell's hired hooligans. The girl was in a different category, and Horne was so impressed by the fact that the dead girl bore no resemblance to a gangster's moll, as he interpreted the phrase, that he was inclined to the belief that the two thugs had picked her up somewhere on the highway and offered her a lift. If that was so, and she was the victim — the innocent victim — of a gang bust-up, the Homicide Bureau was going to stir up plenty of quiz in the precincts of the underworld.

Dr. McTavish had completed his examination of the trio. Horne and Farnes, silenced by the awesomeness of the quiet and sterile morgue, despite their normal preoccupation with such tragedies in the course of their respective duties, bent over the aged doctor to get a glimpse of the body of the dead girl. She had been cleaned up, and now lay, stripped and marble-like, on the cold slab that was her last-but-one resting-place.

Farnes could not resist a low whistle. The dead girl, now looking extremely peaceful and reposed, was like the white marble statue of a Greek Goddess. Her lovely figure lay stretched upon the slab, hands folded underneath her breasts. Her silky hair framed a lovely face: beautiful as any movie star at the height of her fame.

Her eyes had been closed by the doctor, but the long lashes lay smoothly upon her cheeks. Her features were symmetrically perfect, and her partly-opened lips, curved and full, revealed a perfect set of small white, regular teeth. Her full, firm rounded breasts were blue-veined. Her general shape was something to hold Farnes's engrossed attention.

Even Horne seemed to be enthralled by that vision of human loveliness: his eyes grimly regarding the half a dozen wicked-looking wounds where fiendish bullets had ripped into the soft flesh of the silent Madonna. There was a bullet hole in her neck, another in her chest and two grazings across her forehead, by the right temple. Other bullet-holes uglied up her shoulders and arms. Whatever swinish ghouls had poured that stream of bullets into the girl deserved more than the electric chair; they deserved to be slowly tortured to death in the direst agony imaginable. At least, that's how Farnes's mind worked, and he was certain that Horne shared the sentiment.

'What a wicked waste of a girl,' murmured Horne, pensively. 'She was surely out of her mind if she had anything to do with that Cornell mob. A girl like that could make Broadway with her eyes shut. I've never seen a more perfect ensemble.'

Dr. McTavish was not greatly impressed by the obvious charms of his corpse. To him, any dead body was merely a scientific slab of biology, male or female. But, nevertheless, his head nodded slowly as Horne spoke.

Farnes said: 'No idea who she is?'

Horne shrugged. 'Nothing in her purse except a few bucks, a small pistol, some cosmetics and the usual geegaws a woman carries around. No cards, nothing to give a lead to her identity.'

'How about the ugly-looking bruiser from the back seat?'

'Roberts has taken his dabs and picture over to headquarters. We'll know in an hour or two if there's any record on him. I've no doubt there is.'

'Looks like she was with Beamish,' Farnes offered. 'She was in front with him.'

'Might have been a pick-up,' Horne

returned. 'Maybe some girl who hitched a ride across to the mainland. Who knows?'

'Anything on the jalopy?'

'It's not hot, if that's what you mean,' answered Horne.

'That doesn't take you far, then?'

'It takes us no place,' growled Horne. 'I've gotta get the tabs on this girl. Listen, Sandy. I want you to put her picture in the morning edition — front page — with a full description. Someone might identify her. I'll be damned if I'll believe she was mixed up with the Cornell mob.'

Farnes grinned, mirthlessly. 'D'you mean a picture as she is now? You'd get the *Sphere* banned throughout the county.'

'Aw, quit the fool talk, Farnes, for once. I'm too bothered right now to bandy backchat. I'll give you clear pictures of her, head and shoulders, and a description of the clothes she was wearing. I reckon she's about twenty, eh Doc?'

'Near as makes no difference,' McTavish agreed.

''Tis a sorry sight, Lieutenant. She

16

looks mighty like a girl wi' everythin' to live for.'

'Too late for that now,' Farnes murmured. 'The best you can do, lieutenant, is haul in the quick-trigger boy who mussed her pretty body up thataway.'

'And I'll do that,' swore Horne, 'if I have to starve for a fortnight and lose every hour of sleep.'

'Let's have them pictures copper,' Farnes suggested. 'We want to hit the early edition, don't we?'

2

Mick Lomat sauntered through the dressing room door and stood for a moment watching the coloured woman straightening some gowns in the corner. She looked up as he entered and her chubby black face broke into a grin.

'Miss Deane ain't off stage yet, Mister Lomat. Guess you'll wait, huh?' Her broad mouth opened wide, exhibiting large, regular, strong white teeth.

Mike returned the cheery greeting and slapped Mora's hip with the flat of his hand. He was wearing immaculate evening clothes, including a dark homburg and a silk scarf. In his mouth a fat cheroot blazed away like a fire-cracker, emitting thick streams of smoke. He sat down on the edge of the dressing table, regardless of the heavy deposit of powder that smothered the surface.

Mora slid towards the door in her usual waddling manner, thrust it open and went out. In the background, Mick could hear the strains of the tinny orchestra bringing Miss Rita Deane's act to an end with a crescendo. The burst of applause sounded like a thunderclap. Mick smiled to himself.

A moment later she came into the dressing room, slightly breathless, her forehead moist with exertion. Rita Deane always threw herself into her act; she knew that the boys out front liked to hear her melodious voice at high pitch, and to watch her voluptuously contoured body dancing about the stage with primitive abandon.

She had the personality, and she had the shape. Her stage garb was brief, and her high-heeled shoes were uncomfortable and made her stage frolicking a hazardous business, but Rita knew that the higher the heels, the more appealing the poise of the body — and in show business, Rita believed in suffering for her audience.

She wore plenty of jewelry, several rings on her fingers, a diamond anklet on her right leg, two bangles, and a paste necklet. These she pulled off now and threw on to the dressing table, seemingly oblivious to Mick's presence.

'Hiya, honey,' said Mick, appraising her body with wide eyes. 'I wouldn't take those trinkets off, sweetheart. You might catch pneumonia.'

'What are you doin' here?' Rita demanded, aloofly.

'We had a date remember?'

'I never remember,' she returned, slipping behind the tapestry screen out of Mick's view. A moment later a brassiere was thrown over the top of the screen, followed a second later by stockings and tights. Mick watched the shadowy silhouette on the wall, and continued speaking.

'Where d'you want to go, honey? Just name the dive and we can be there in two shakes.'

When she appeared from behind the screen, she was wearing a dark embroidered kimono. As she came towards the dressing table, Mick pulled her into his arms. She resisted without any real effort.

'Don't mess about now, Mike. I've got

to get dressed. Buzz off to the bar and I'll meet you later.'

He kissed her firmly on the lips. Her smooth cheek rested for a moment against his and she felt the pressure of his hands across her back. He looked into her eyes, savoring the depth of their violet hue and the long lashes. His eyes regarded her loveliness with acute desire and Rita began to push him away.

'On your way, Mike. I don't want to be here all night.'

He drew away, releasing her.

'Okay. I'll go and get a small rye. But for Pete's sake snap into it.'

He went out, closing the door noisily. Rita pursed her moist red lips and flicked her hands among the gowns in the wardrobe, seeking something suitable for her night out.

As she dressed, slowly and languorously, she considered again the proposal which the theatrical agent, Sol Podman had made just before the show that evening. Sol was rehearsing a new burlesque in conjunction with a big backer named Fortescue, an English

21

variety producer. Fortescue had seen Rita at the Avery Burlesque, and wanted her to star in the new production. Rita didn't object to advancement, but on the other hand, she had worked with Miles Young, the owner of the Avery Burlesque Theatre, for three years and she felt that she owed him a certain amount of loyalty. She knew that she alone was responsible for the huge success the Avery enjoyed; packed houses night after night.

The contract Sol offered was not to be ignored. It would give her the chance to make some real money, instead of having to parade her torso every night in front of a bunch of pie-eyed and pop-eyed guys, and earn peanuts. The Avery show was fifth-rate and she knew it. Her salary was good, of its kind. But Sol had offered her the big chance — the opportunity to star in a new burlesque show which would tour the big cities.

She climbed into the low-cut satin gown and smoothed it over her delectable body, admiring the effect in the pier-glass.

Then she sat down and busied herself

with the jars and bottles that littered the dressing table.

Ten minutes or so later she joined Mick Lomat in the bar. He was on his fifth rye and looked impatient.

'Gee, it takes you a hell of a time to get ready, baby, but the effect's worth every second of it!' he admired.

'Get me a drink,' said Rita, sighing. 'I've got something on my mind, Mike. I've got to think.'

He ordered a Martini and repeated his call for more rye.

They sat on the high stools, Mike sneaking glances at her while she studiously contemplated the future. Whether to accept Sol's offer of a contract, or whether to stick with dear old Miles.

'If you're gonna sit there wilting,' Mike said ruefully, 'I'm gonna take a peep at the racing results.'

He hauled an evening paper out of his pocket and folded it across the bar top. His eyes searched the columns for several seconds, while he sipped his drink. Rita had sunk herself into a deep reverie.

As he straightened out the paper again, searching for the other sport's results, the inner fold of the paper fell to the floor and lay flat just at Rita's feet. She glanced down, a sarcastic comment ready on her lips, just as Mike slid off his stool and bent to retrieve the sheet. Then, abruptly, Rita's demeanor underwent a change. She jumped off the stool and snatched the paper from Mike's fingers, almost knocking him over. Her eyes were transfixed on the two center columns at the top of the sheet, where a picture of a young girl's head and shoulders was printed below the heavy headlines reading:

**'Mystery Moll in Gang Shooting.
Unknown Beauty in
Island Triple Murder.'**

Mike, frowning heavily, saw how her hands trembled as she held the sheet.

'Anything botherin' you, honey?' he murmured.

She didn't reply. Her eyes were scanning the columns of the report. Mike leaned over and read it with her.

The report was a re-write from a city paper, morning edition. It covered the discovery of the stationary jalopy on the island highway, and the finding of the three riddled bodies. The police had identified one of the men — the dead driver — as Peter Beamish, thirty-five year old 'king' of the Kitkat Club on Tenth Avenue. The other man and the dead woman were still unidentified. The theory was that the three victims had been shot by members of a rival gang, since it was well known that Pete Beamish was a close friend of Woolf Cornell, the racketeer. Comment was made bearing upon the previous shooting of Lynx Larsen, another member of the Cornell organization. The police were concerned in case these shootings heralded yet another flare up of vicious gang-warfare and the Metropolitan forces had been notified to stay on tip-toe.

The biggest paragraph was about the unknown girl. A beautiful and attractively-dressed girl of about twenty. There was not the slightest clue to her identity but the police thought she might be one of the women known to hang around the Kitkat precincts and to be mixed up with the Cornell outfit.

Mike grunted: 'Nasty business, Babe. She looks a swell piece of goods. I guess . . . '

'Shut up!' Rita snapped. 'Let's get out of here.'

She crushed the paper in her hands and still hanging onto it, stormed angrily out of the bar. Mike followed hastily, filled with perplexity.

He caught up with her on the sidewalk.

'Call a cab,' Rita commanded.

Mike shrugged. He hailed a passing cab and they climbed aboard.

'What's eatin' you, Rita?' asked Mike, with concern. 'You're actin' mighty queer? Was there anythin' in that blurb that upset you . . . ?'

'Mike,' she said, her teeth clenched. 'I've gotta go up to town. I've got to drop everything. I want you to help me.'

'Why, sure, sure,' Mike growled. 'Anythin' you say, honey. But what is all this?'

'Never mind that now. I've gotta get

away. Take me to my apartment and help me pack a few things.'

'But what about our date?'

'That's off,' she snapped. 'Don't you understand, I'm in trouble.'

'In trouble?' he echoed, mystified.

'Well, not me. I've got trouble, that's what I mean. It's the same thing. I've gotta find something out.'

'It's something to do with that shootin', eh?'

'It's *everythin'* to do with that,' she acknowledged.

He was amazed at the change in her. She seemed older, more violent, more vindictive than he had ever known her. She spat out her words and her face was drawn into a most fierce expression.

'That picture,' she said, harshly. 'That's my sister. My kid sister Pat.'

For a moment her announcement silenced him. Then he said:

'Are you sure? But how come . . . ?'

'I don't know anythin' about it at the moment. I haven't heard from Pat in months. Last time I heard from her she was working at a steady job in New Jersey

27

and had a boyfriend stuck on her. They were plannin' to get married. I was figurin' on takin' a vacation with her next month. It's maybe six, seven months since I last heard from her. I don't know what all this is about . . . but my sister was never a gunman's moll. That's definite. There's some mystery about this an' I'm gonna find out what it's all about.'

'You might have made a mistake,' suggested Mike.

'I don't think so,' muttered Rita. 'The picture was clear enough, an' anyway, there was a description of her.'

Mike bunched his teeth:

'Listen, honey,' he said. 'Don't do anythin' rash. Maybe I'd better come with you, huh?'

'I know what I'm doing,' Rita retorted, savagely. 'I can handle this alone. If those mugs have dragged my kid sister into anythin' I'll . . . '

'Be sensible, Babe,' Mike implored. 'If your sister was mixed up with those hoodlums, you'll be sticking your neck into a police job.'

'If they killed my sister,' Rita choked,

'I'll tear them apart. I gotta find out what this is all about. There's something.'

Mike interrupted her, gripping her arm roughly.

'Listen, you young fool,' he snapped. 'You might have made a mistake. Before you start gettin' tough you'd better check that it *is* your sister.'

'That's what I intend to do,' she replied, shaking herself free of his grasp. 'Pat wasn't the sort of kid to get into trouble.' Suddenly she burst into tears. 'It's my fault, if anythin' happened to the kid. I was supposed to be takin' care of her.'

The cab hauled up at her apartment.

Mike paid off the driver and followed Rita upstairs.

3

Woolf Cornell sat heavily on the chair behind his desk in the Kitkat Office, upstairs at the rear of the Club. He was a thick-set, burly guy, with broad shoulders, a terrific girth, and possessed a most hideous face — large ears, high domed forehead, thick bushy eyebrows over closely-set, beady eyes, a grossly flattened and bulbous tipped nose, thick, sensuous, wet lips. From his mouth drooped a black cigar as fat as his thumb on his large hand.

There was nothing in the office to suggest what business Cornell carried on: the smaller office downstairs possessed the atmosphere of a Club sanctum, but Cornell's big, airy room upstairs was void of hints as to his undertakings. It was furnished impressively, so much so that it might have been the office of a wealthy stockbroker or a bank manager. The walls were bare, except for one large map of the district, and the filing boxes and steel safes were quite unadorned, unlabeled and suspiciously unused. There was a battery of telephones on the desk, and in one corner stood a white fountain of ice water.

Cornell was not alone: he had a visitor. A tall, slim, gaunt-looking man, dressed in loose-fitting clothes that gave him a hungry look. His soft felt hat was still on his head, tilted across his forehead. He was smoking a tired-looking cigarette, and gazing at Cornell through the haze of blue smoke.

One peculiarity of Cornell's was his innate composure. He sat serenely, relaxed, his forehead smooth as a babe's shoulder. His voice was a drooling, drawling undertone which carried a hint of his ruthlessness and decisiveness of character.

'I'm replacing Beamish with Vallant,' he said.

'Yeah, yeah, that's all very well. One of the boys gets slugged and you replace him. It sounds perfectly natural and businesslike,' complained the other. 'But I tell ya we've gotta do something. Something quick. This shooting business is no coincidence. Someone's hornin' in on this district, Cornell, and we gotta protect our interests.'

Cornell poured himself a glass of bourbon, using a bottle which came from one of the drawers in his desk. His movements were slow and deliberate, and when he replied to the other guy, his voice still contained no emotion.

'I'm quite aware of the situation, Gyler,' he observed.

'None of us are safe,' Gyler protested. 'Whatever outfit is behind this knows the strength.'

'Naturally,' Cornell drawled. 'But you forget, Gyler, that I ain't exactly asleep. Don't worry your pretty head about a couple of killings. We'll deal with that in good time. I believe in playing safe — making certain. It ain't to my likin' to act just yet. I'm waiting for somethin'.'

'Waitin',' snapped the tall man. 'Waitin's dangerous. An' your figures ain't right, either. There's been *four* killin's. Larsen, Pete Beamish, Guppy the Grid

— and don't forget the dame.'

'Ah, yes. The dame. That *was* unfortunate,' declared Cornell. 'A great pity. She was a very sweet piece of goods, Gyler. I had some pretty big ideas for that babe.'

'Yeah, I don't doubt it,' said Gyler, superciliously. 'But it's put the coppers off balance and they're asking more questions than's natural. I always said it was a mistake to have anythin' to do with that dame. She ain't gonna be forgotten all that quick by the coppers, and another thing — she never was cut out for our kind of racket. She was just a sweet innocent kid, an' she oughta've been left alone . . . '

'Sometimes,' sighed Cornell, dropping a stream of ash into the tray, 'you get in my hair, Gyler. I'm sorry about the dame, naturally. But it was unfortunate. We never expected what happened. I'm just as burned up over the loss of Pete — but there's nothin' we can do to remedy the losses. All we c'n do is take action against this muscler when the right time comes. But that ain't yet, Gyler — not yet. I know what I'm doin'.'

'Guppy the Grid was a big loss,' Gyler said, pointedly. 'And Larsen, too. Two of our best men. This rat behind those killings ain't pottin' our boys off haphazard. He knows what he's doin'.'

'That,' returned Cornell, 'is why you're fairly safe, Gyler. You're only the guy who takes care of the books. It's the guys with the quick-trigger fingers that our friend is aimin' at. You can sleep nice and quiet, Gyler. And me, too, for the time bein'. Y'see, Gyler, I've got a pretty shrewd idea of the guy's plan. I guess I've figured out exactly what the game is. And I'm playin' this my way. As far as your worries concerning the recent over-conscientiousness of the police department, all you have to do is keep the books like we want 'em. You don't know nothin', and you ain't interested in anythin' except your own work — see? That's the line you have to take with the coppers, and that's as much as you need to tell 'em. So quit excercisin' your tongue and quit botherin' your pretty head. Now beat it back to the house and carry on as though nothin' happened. There's bound to be a lot of police quizzin' for the next few days. Just ignore it and keep your mouth closed outside of anythin' to do with the accounts.'

Gyler pursed his lips.

'Okay,' he grunted. 'But I still don't like it. I figure this other mob is out to liquidate your organization and I didn't figure on bein' a target for a stream of slugs when I took the job on . . . '

'Took the job on?' smiled Cornell, sneeringly. 'If I hadn't pulled you out of that embezzlement shemozzle you were in with Lingfield's you'd be doin' a pretty good job on a rockery right now, and don't you ever forget it. Your lily skin's safe enough, I tell you. Now beat it, and get back to work.'

'Okay,' snapped Gyler, and turning on his heels quit the room. The moment he'd gone Cornell switched a button on the desk. A squat, ugly-looking little man came in from the adjoining room.

'Gyler's just left,' said Cornell. 'He's got the jitters about the recent shootin'. Seems like Beamish and Guppy's deaths upset the poor guy. He's liable to do a run-out and he might not have any scruples about the records over at the house. Get over there and keep an eye on him. If he acts suspiciously in any way, you know what to do. We can't afford to have any yellow-bellies on the team right now.'

'You said it, Mr. Cornell,' nodded the squat man.

He vanished as silently as he'd appeared. For a moment or two Cornell sat staring out of the window, ruminating. Then he stood up, gave another glance out of the window, and moved towards the other door, leading to the corridor that linked the rear of the premises to the front of the building where the Club was housed.

It was early yet, and the Club was quiet. In the foyer two of the cuties who acted as waitresses were chatting with the hat-check girl. All three were dressed in the spangled tights and brief costumes effected by the female staff on the Club floor. The band was tuning up. Only two or three tables were occupied, but there were half a dozen people in the cocktail bar. Cornell nodded to the big guy standing just inside the main entrance: he had a suspicious bulge under his tuxedo jacket. Cornell walked through the foyer and made for the office.

Inside two men were waiting for him. One of these, the younger and more presentable man, was Bruce Vallant, an ex-con who was a specialist in jewelry and had perfected his own system of relieving wealthy socialites of their heirlooms. In San Francisco Vallant could never have held down a job like the one Cornell had promoted him to — manager of the Kitkat. He was fairly well-known to every nightspot patron on the coast. But on the Atlantic coast he was as good as new, and Cornell was glad to have him on his strength.

'Everything all right, Vallant?' Cornell demanded, sitting at the small bureau and watching the two men closely.

'Yeah. I guess so.'

'You're not worried about the fact that Beamish got his?'

'Not particularly,' replied Vallant. 'I reckon Beamish was unfortunate. The mob was after Guppy. Beamish and the

37

dame just happened to be in a tight spot.'

'That's one way to see it,' nodded Cornell. 'And you needn't worry about retaliation because we're workin' on that right now. For the time being Freedsom here will keep on your tail in case anythin' looks like breakin' — an' I dare say you know how good Freedsom is with a Luger, huh?'

Freedsom grinned. He was a slightly-built, fresh-complexioned little fellow with a broad, flashing grin that showed up his perfectly regular white teeth to advantage.

Vallant said: 'Yeah. I heard. I'll be glad to have him around.'

'I'm havin' a meetin' upstairs at half-past eleven. I'd like you to be there, Vallant. It concerns the shootings of Larsen and Guppy the Grid. You'll be on the rota with Podge, Freedsom, and there'll be two other guys watchin' the back. As regards the show here Vallant, Beamish had everythin' nicely organized, so the take-over shouldn't give you much trouble. Anythin' you ain't sure about, refer to me. Okay?'

'Okay,' Vallant nodded.

'There'll be a lot of quizzin' from the police department,' Cornell observed. 'Seems the death of that dame got in among their hair. Normally they wouldn't have taken a great deal of trouble over the death of Guppy, and Beamish too for that matter. But the dame's got 'em puzzled and they're still checkin'. You know nothin' about her, if you understand? Let the cops talk to me if they want to know anythin'.'

'Funny she ain't been identified yet,' put in Freedsom. 'Reckon that name she operated under was a phoney — maybe she's not the lonely orphan she played at, eh? That might make for trouble, eh?'

'Anyone'd think we weren't used to trouble in this business' drawled Cornell, staring into Freedsom's narrowed eyes.

'Sure,' Freedsom returned, 'but I . . . '

'Aw, forget it,' snapped Cornell. 'It was just a bad turn-up, that's all. No one figured anything'd happen to that dame did they?'

'Maybe not,' Freedsom allowed, 'but it's a nasty business, Chief. I don't like it.

39

She ain't — wasn't — one of them floosies we generally get around here . . . '

'Well, it was an accident, wasn't it?' Cornell said. 'The dame must have known what kind of game Beamish was mixed up in. How were we to know she was just usin' him. Until we learned about her connection with that young Stratton guy, we figured she was just interested in Beamish. We'd have taken care of her some different way if she hadn't got herself killed like she did. It wasn't our fault she happened to be with Beamish and Guppy that night.'

Vallant said: 'Did you manage to locate young Stratton anyplace?'

Cornell shook his head: 'Nope,' he admitted, 'but we'll find him. He might show up now that he knows the dame's dead. He'll have watched the papers, I guess.'

'He's gonna be good and sore,' said Freedsom.

'He's a kid,' snapped Cornell. 'I reckon we can take care of a kid, can't we?'

Neither of the other two men vouch-safed an answer.

Cornell grunted and stood up.

'I'll be around for another half hour or so. Don't forget the meetin' tonight.'

He went out into the Club again. Freedsom turned to Vallant and grinned: 'Sometimes I reckon the chief kinda had a soft spot for that young dame himself. The way his eyes popped the first time he saw her in Beamish's office — in this very office — would have made a chorus-girl blush.'

Vallant didn't say anything. His thoughts turned back to the first time he himself had seen the girl who had called herself 'Honey' Delmar. She had visited the Club once or twice, in company with different men. Then one night she had come alone. Beamish had taken a tumble for her, and the girl had apparently reciprocated his feelings. For some time the two of them had been as close as sardines in a can — but Vallant knew that the girl was ignorant of Beamish's real life. She figured he was just a Club manager. Vallant had been as jealous as every other guy in the Club. 'Honey' Delmar was the snappiest, most provocatively gorgeous female they'd seen around in many years.

Vallant had danced with her the first night she had visited the Kitkat. He still remembered, with something of an ache, the closeness of her fresh young body as she danced lightly in his arms: her captivating beauty had turned his blood to molten metal and set fire to every nerve fiber.

Her death had come as a shock to Vallant. The very day of the shooting in the sedan, Cornell had learned something of the truth behind the young girl's apparently innocent visits to the Kitkat. She was young Jim Stratton's girl! Stratton, who had got into financial difficulties and borrowed money from Cornell in return for a small service.

The firm for which Stratton worked was a company manufacturing commercial chemical products. Cornell had wanted drugs — a quantity of drugs to fill a contract he'd made for which the illegal consignment had been snatched and confiscated. The matter was urgent — the goods had to be shipped at a certain date.

Stratton, in Cornell's debt, had been compelled to get the drugs — to steal them from the factory. It had been a tough job to pull off, but he had succeeded in part. He'd got the stuff for Cornell, and had been discovered. Since then he'd been on the run, wanted by the police for questioning in connection with the removal of valuable and dangerous drugs from the factory.

For some weeks after the young man had vanished Cornell had been trying to locate him, intending to give him a break — to let Stratton join up with his organization. Then 'Honey' Delmar had turned up. Until the morning of her death in Beamish's sedan, no one had suspected her connection with the missing youngster, but one of Cornell's men had found out the truth. 'Honey' Delmar and Beamish had left that morning for a drive across to Hope Island, taking Guppy the Grid along. Vallant now knew that Guppy had been sent by Cornell to keep an eye on Beamish and the girl, because Cornell had a suspicion that Beamish might be harboring some reforming notions.

News of the killing of the three occupants of the car had come through that night; Cornell had already prepared his plan of campaign for dealing with the girl. He knew now that she was evidently trying to get something on the Cornell outfit — probably some inside information concerning the shipping of the drugs — for Stratton.

Now, 'Honey' Delmar — or whatever her real name was — was as cold as a shoulder of mutton; killed by the mob opposing Cornell on the East territory.

It was a sickening business and it had Vallant as worried as some of the others in the outfit. The cops would naturally take a greater interest in the girl's death than they would in the deaths of Beamish and Guppy — because the cops were quite used to gang slayings, and even welcomed them because they served a semi-social purpose. Indeed there were some regulars who would have welcomed a great free-for-all between the rival gangs, ending in their complete annihilation. The law aside, most cops were mighty pleased to read about gang slayings.

Someone knocked on the office door and thrust Vallant's memories to one side. He hurled out a curt: 'Yes, who is it?' and settled down to the business of stepping into Beamish's shoes.

4

Cornell's office, upstairs, was crowded with men and the smoke lay thick on the air from a mixture of cigars, cheroots and cigarettes. The stench of liquor permeated the atmosphere.

Cornell had already gone into complete details regarding the presence in town of an 'opposition party', but by and large he seemed peculiarly unperturbed. He explained that from the Middle West had come a wise-guy by the name of Tony Molari, whose ancestors emanated from sunny Italy. Molari seemed to imagine that because he had achieved a somewhat notorious reputation in Chicago, he would be able to transfer his influence quite easily to the coast-board, and muscle in on a territory which had for the past four or five years been the unapproachable province of Cornell and his mob. The cops had finally made it too hot for Molari in Chicago, so he'd packed his bags and lit out for the bright lights of the Atlantic coast, bringing with him a bevy of strong-arm boys and a small team of ruthless quick-trigger lugs. At first Molari had gone easy. He'd had to get the lie of the land and discover who was who around town. It hadn't taken him overlong to reach the conclusion that the only guy who mattered was Cornell, whose mob was a strong organization controlling every avenue of graft and vice in an area of many square miles.

'Now,' went on Cornell, 'if there's one thing this lug Molari has to his credit, it's a particularly interesting system of protection — the protection racket which was born and bred in the Middle West. So far we haven't had the organization nor the experience to run such a racket alongside our normal business. Okay, here's where we put one over on Molari and make him serve us a useful purpose, see?'

Several of the men, Vallant among them, confessed that they did not see.

'It's plain enough,' grinned Cornell, smoothly. 'We give Molari enough rope.

We let him get entrenched. We let him believe that he's becoming another big-shot around here. And we let him start operations, particularly in the protection racket line which until now we've steered clear of. And then — when he's got everything nice and tidy, all neatly organized and smoothly running — well, that's when we step in! Instead of Molari muscling in on our operations, *we* step into his racket and take over. That's easy enough to understand ain't it?'

There was a moment's silence while this information seeped into the dim brains of some of the less intelligent members of the organization. Vallant broke the silence eventually to declare:

'Yeah, it's a very neat idea, Chief, but surely we ain't gonna sit around meanwhile and watch this mug snipe off our boys one at a time? Something's gotta be done about *that*.'

All eyes were now turned on Cornell: watchful and keen eyes. Cornell threw a glance around the room.

'Yeah, I know,' he said easily. 'I figure that these recent shootings of Molari's were just kind of visiting cards to announce his arrival in town and to make us think he has a strong organization. The facts are that his few lugs are still gettin' their bearings. They don't offer a great deal of opposition at the moment, but Molari's figurin' on attractin' a few of our boys onto his team. There's big pickin's in the protection racket: some of you guys might find a proposition of that sort interestin'. But on the other hand,' he said, with a wealth of meaning, 'I don't reckon on many of you lugs takin' a powder on this outfit as long as we're still powerful enough to run the town's sideshows, huh? And that's gonna be for a long, long time yet.'

Vallant insisted: 'But what about these snipings, Chief? What are we gonna do about them? I reckon we oughta show our hand. It oughta be easy enough to locate the trigger boys who pulled off those two shootings. I suggest . . . '

Cornell silenced him with a curt reminder.

'I'm still the boss around here, Vallant. If there's any suggestin' to be done, I reckon I'll continue to do it for a while, huh?'

'Okay,' snapped Vallant, 'but that still doesn't rule out what I said. Something's gotta be done about Larsen and Beamish and Guppy . . . '

Cornell interrupted again. 'You guys all seem to think I'm asleep most of the time. You can quit frettin', all of you. I've got two guys out now checkin' on the latest moves Molari is making. There's not a move he makes we don't know about. It might interest you to know now that Lynx Larsen was already plannin' to double-cross us — Molari had offered him a spot bang in the center of his protection set-up, and Larsen always was a guy who looked for the big pickings. He was shot by Molari's outfit because Molari got last-minute jitters that Larsen might turn the tables and play for both sides at once. That much I know from something Guppy the Grid found out.'

'Guppy?' exclaimed Vallant.

'Yeah, Guppy,' repeated Cornell. 'I know what's goin' on around here all the time, you lugs, so don't you ever figure anythin' different.' He gave them all a searching stare. Then he added: 'It may be that Guppy was singled out by Molari for the pay-off because of his snooping. Molari might have got wise to what was going on between Guppy and one of his own boys, but Guppy wasn't playing any double-cross. He was checkin' on Larsen. It's just unfortunate that I had to send Guppy with Beamish that afternoon when Beamish went across to the island with the dame. I had a notion the floosie might have been puttin' ideas into Beamish's noodle. That's why I always tell you guys not to have any truck with dames. They're sheer poison. You never know when they're going to pull some stunt that'll shove you on a morgue slab.'

Vallant said: 'That makes things look a bit different. Maybe Beamish was never meant to collect those slugs . . . '

'It's too late to talk about that — he's had his quota,' Cornell observed with brutal indifference. 'The reason I fetched you all here tonight was to wise you up concerning the general set-up in case any of you were gettin' the jitters over Molari.

So now you know. You don't have to lose any sleep. Although the rat doesn't know it himself, he's only workin' away at a project that's gonna add more strength to our organization as soon as we're ready to take action.'

There was a murmur of conversation among the collected mobsters, and over the hubbub came the buzzing of a bell on Cornell's desk. The chief flicked a button on the two-way talkie and a voice said:

'Mr. Vallant's wanted in the Club Office.'

Cornell turned to Vallant.

'Someone to see you, Vallant. There's not much we've got to talk about. You'd better go down and see what's cookin'.'

Vallant nodded and quit the room. As the door closed Cornell began to detail some of the men to certain jobs which were lined up. Some of the men were dismissed in ones and twos, until only Cornell and the squat little man named Podge remained in the room.

Podge wore his enduring grin, the red scar across his right cheek glowing hideously in the artificial light.

Cornell said: 'When Atkin and Morell show up, have them report to me at the house. I'm goin' back and get me a bath. I feel kind of grimy. It's maybe from bein' around so many bums all at one time. Is the car ready?'

'Sure, boss,' replied Podge. 'I filled the tank earlier on tonight.'

'Okay. You can blow now. I've got some telephonin' to do.'

Podge was just about to make his exit when the buzzer rang again on Cornell's desk. He flipped the button and asked curtly: 'Yeah? What is it?'

Across the wire came the distant voice of Vallant from the Club office.

'There's someone here wants to see you, chief.'

'Who is it? If it's the police department tell 'em I'll be available at home within the next hour. This is a fine time of the night to come . . . '

'It ain't that,' said Vallant, breaking into the chief's outburst. 'It's a dame.'

'A dame?' Cornell inquired. 'What dame?' His voice became less harsh 'One of the patrons?'

'Nope. Some dame lookin' for a job.'

'This time of night?' snapped Cornell. 'Tell her to see me in the mornin'.'

'I already told her. She figures maybe you'll see her tonight. Seems she just blew into town and she has no place to go nor anythin'. Reckons she could add to the cabaret attraction at the Club. I wouldn't've bothered you, Chief, but she looks like she might make the grade.'

'You know we ain't hirin' no more showgirls,' Cornell said. 'I thought you'd be able to handle that side of the business without pesterin' me with every darned little job of work that crops up. If you think you need another girl for the show and she meets the bill, hire her. If not, sling her out.'

'It ain't that easy, Chief,' Vallant murmured. 'She's determined to see you if she has to sit around the office all night.'

'Uh. One of those, eh? What kind of a manager are you if you can't . . . '

'She's not a bad looker,' Vallant observed. 'There's no spot in the show wants fillin', but this dame reckons she has what it takes. She does a song and dance routine. Comes from some burlesque outfit out of town. Maybe she had reason to turn up missin'.'

'What kind of shape's she got?' asked Cornell.

'I ain't seen any better,' confided Vallant.

Cornell was silent for a moment. He drummed his fingers on the desk. Then Vallant said: 'I thought maybe you *ought* to see her, Chief. You'll know what I mean then.'

'Uh-huh,' grunted Cornell. 'Okay. I c'n give her three minutes. Send her up.'

'I'll bring her up,' Vallant declared, closing off.

Four minutes later he entered Cornell's room, bundling a young woman into the private sanctum. Cornell was toying with some papers at the desk, pretending to be immersed in some acute problem connected with the Club's affairs. He glanced up and turned his eyes back to the papers automatically. Then his eyes seemed to open several inches wider and he stared rudely at the visitor.

His gaze started at her feet and wandered inquisitively up towards her hat. Then he reversed the examination and started to stroke his nose.

'You can go, Vallant,' he commanded, smoothly.

Vallant frowned. He caught Cornell's severe glare and unprotestingly, yet with evident reluctance, he went out again.

'You too Podge,' said Cornell, indicating the door to Podge who had lingered during Vallant's internal-phone call.

Podge nodded, grinning broadly, and slid towards the door, his eyes also making an appraising survey of the visitor.

'Sit down,' Cornell said. 'What's your name?'

'Betty Fox,' came the reply, sweetly. 'But they call me 'Bubbles' in the business.'

'The business?'

'The show,' she explained. 'My act is a bubble dance. Y'know — with balloons. Sometimes with soap suds. I've also worked with pigeons and doves but they're kind of temperamental. I once got let down pretty badly by a couple of pigeons.'

Cornell smiled.

'I bet that was discomforting,' he suggested.

'The boys out front didn't seem to mind,' she confessed.

'So you want a job?' quizzed Cornell, his eyes riveted to her shapely legs.

'That's right,' she answered. 'I had to blow town on account of some trouble I had with a boyfriend. I heard that you were a guy who didn't ask too many questions.'

'You heard that huh?'

'Yeah. I guess your fame has spread around a little.'

'That's nice to know,' admitted Cornell, suspiciously.

'I had a top spot with a first-rate burlesque company. Filled the house night after night. It was a good job and I hated to leave it. But maybe you could use a good act for your Club? That's what I figured.'

'Could be,' said Cornell. She loosed off her wrap and revealed herself dressed in a clinging tulle gown, designed off the shoulders and cut low on the bodice. Cornell stared at her admiringly. Her skin was satin smooth, pinkly fresh in the glare of the light. Her glossy hair, loose and exquisitely waved framed a very handsome face, with a neat aquiline nose, large, clear, green eyes and two full and moist red lips. When she spoke, smilingly, she showed her small white regular teeth. Cornell was impressed. More than that, he was beginning to feel the impact of the girl's presence. The perfume she affected was beginning to counter the lingering smells of cigarette and liquor. Its delectable and feminine flavor began to have an effect on Cornell's sweat glands. Normally he had little interest in women: there were always a dozen or more hanging around the Club and the pick of them were his for the waggle of a finger. He had grown to mistrust and dislike women as women, and only bothered with them at all for the animal pleasure he was able to extort from them. But this girl was different with a capital D.

Cornell said, softly: 'Well, if you want a

job, let's see what you've got to offer. Let's see you dance a couple of steps.'

Obligingly Miss Fox tripped a few light fantastics around the office, humming a tune under her breath. Her voice was soft and resonant.

'I guess you'd be all right,' Cornell enthused, slowly. 'When can you start work?'

'As soon as you say,' 'Bubbles' answered. 'I told you the jam I'm in. No place to go, and no one in town I can . . . '

'You short of dough?' inquired Cornell.

'No. Not for the moment. I've got a few bucks to see me through. I'll take an apartment tomorrow. I c'n check into one of the hotels for tonight.'

'That,' said Cornell, watching her intently, 'may not be necessary.' He was silent for a few seconds, then said, 'I reckon you an' me ought to get a little better acquainted, Miss Fox. Then I c'n tell you something about the work here, and the kind of people you're likely to meet. This — this trouble you're in — it don't concern the cops, does it? I mean . . . '

'Gee no,' said the girl, hastily. 'I told you — it's like I said. There was a man involved . . . I just had to skip town.'

'His wife turned up?' Cornell suggested slyly.

'Well — sort of,' she admitted, reluctantly.

'Too bad,' said Cornell, rising to his feet and stubbing the two inches of his cigar in the tray. He moved across the room and stood in front of her. She could feel the vibration of his pulse, almost.

'I thought maybe you'd like to see one of the other dives around town,' said Cornell. 'It ain't too late yet. Maybe you could use a spot of food, huh?'

'Well, I haven't eaten in some hours,' she said, watching him. His hand moved into hers, and then slowly he caressed her wrist.

'How about the Sprobeck Club?' he said.

'I don't know any of the joints around here.'

'It's not bad. The food's eatable.'

'But aren't you very busy?' she asked.

'Yeah, but it'll keep. I pay other guys to

do the donkey work around here,' he answered.

'Yeah. I heard you were quite a big-shot in town,' she mused.

'You seem to have heard a lot about me, honey,' he drawled.

'Yeah,' she breathed, her eyes fixed on his glassy expression. His breathing was becoming more difficult. She knew that she was having the same effect on Cornell that she had on all other men between the ages of sixteen and sixty with whom she came into contact.

'Slip your wrap on. It gets chilly, nights,' Cornell told her. 'My car's in the alley. We can go down the back stairs.'

'I left my luggage at the depot,' she said.

'We'll collect it on the way,' he said.

'I changed into this get-up on your backstage,' she informed him. 'Hadn't I better collect my clothes from down there first?'

'You c'n pick 'em up tomorrow,' Cornell replied. 'If you're short of anythin' I c'n arrange an advance on your salary. You can do some buyin' tomorrow.'

'Talkin' of salary,' Miss Fox demurred. 'We didn't discuss any figure.'

'That's right,' Cornell nodded. 'Let's say a hundred bucks a week for a start. If you knock the patrons for a sell-out, I'll make it five hundred.'

She smiled, but he couldn't determine whether it was a smile of approval or approbation. He ignored it, as though his quotation was final. He said:

'That settles that. Now let's go.'

'Okay,' she said.

He bundled her through the door and along the short passage leading to the rear of the building. Down one flight of dusty stairs, along another corridor, and then down a final flight of steps that brought them to ground level, in a narrow mews, beside the Club. The strains of music and other noises, muffled, came to them as they crossed the cobbled stones towards the shining black Packard parked beside the one solitary lamp in the narrow street.

'Kind of dreary out here, isn't it?' murmured 'Bubbles,' feeling that she must say something.

'Sure is,' nodded Cornell, opening the

door for her. 'The glamor's all on the other side. It cost plenty to fix up this joint, I c'n tell you, Baby. Plenty.'

A moment later they were driving at a fast pace along the waterfront, and then they turned in towards the city limits. The highway stretched out before them and the city lights were a distant haze.

Bubbles said: 'How far is this Club you mentioned?'

Cornell turned to her and grinned.

'I changed my mind,' he said. 'We ain't goin'.'

'Oh. Then . . . ?'

'I thought you'd maybe like it better at my place. I can get a proper meal fixed there and we can be more comfortable. I like being comfortable,' he confided, salaciously.

'Yeah,' returned Betty Fox, eyeing him distrustfully. 'I can believe that.'

'Don't worry, Babe,' he urged. 'You ain't going be troubled any. I guess you an' me will get along fine together. I kind of took a likin' to you the first time I saw you.'

'You did?'

'Sure. You've got what it takes.'

'I bet you've got quite a lot of women interested in you Mr. Cornell,' she commented.

'Nope,' came the answer. 'As a matter of fact I ain't interested in women generally. I always tell my boys they're poison. But you're kind of different.'

'That's nice of you, Mr. Cornell,' she said, cautiously.

'Yeah,' Cornell said, almost to himself. 'I reckon you an' me'll get along swell. Settle back and relax, honey. It's quite a stretch to my place. Big joint, over on the west side. You'll like it.'

'Betty Fox' settled back in the luxurious depths of the limousine as it purred silently through the night.

She thought to herself: 'Well, here it is, Rita my pippin. You didn't lose any time getting into the thick of things. This is Cornell. Play your cards right and you won't be long finding out just where poor Pat figured in the set-up. Someone with a knife in Cornell's organization bumped off those three in that green sedan, and my kid sister got killed just when her whole life might have been beginning to be worth living . . . '

With which thoughts Rita Deane troubled her mind until the motion of the car gradually lulled her into a state of drowsiness, helped by the long journey she had undertaken that afternoon. She dropped asleep just a few minutes before the big Packard pulled to a halt outside the rambling old country house where Cornell's main headquarters were installed.

5

Rita played her cards with the determination and intensity of a woman thirsting for vengeance: she was gripped in a passion of wild fury, her whole body tensed inwardly, her entire nervous system frozen with acute hatred for the men responsible for the death of her kid sister. Every action she made, every word she spoke, was part of her plan — a plan so far incomplete, but the motive running like a firm obsession through her mind constantly: to bring about the destruction of those who had struck down Pat.

She knew that Cornell was to blame only in so far as he had somehow been responsible for Pat's connection with the organization. Soon enough she discovered that Beamish had been the man singled out by Pat for her main attractions. And although Rita did not know everything about her sister, she knew her personality and nature well enough to realize that Pat would never have done the dirty on her boyfriend.

Even six months earlier Pat had written to Rita very enthusiastically about 'Jimmy' — Jimmy Stratton — whom she hoped to marry.

Without knowing any of the main details, Rita theorized that Pat must have had some reason for cultivating the association with Beamish and the Cornell group. It was her first job to discover what had happened to Stratton and then to learn why Pat had met her death in the way she had. Rita dismissed all thoughts suggesting that Pat could have had any sinister connection with the mob. She wanted to find out the whole truth, and then to destroy the men who were responsible.

So far her acting had been superb. She had ingratiated herself right into the center of the gangsters' stronghold and had become, within a few days, the privileged girlfriend of the big-shot Cornell himself.

For a couple of days Cornell played along slowly and with as much grace as his gross mind and body would permit.

He discovered that 'Bubbles' Fox was set to become a firm favorite with the Kitkat patrons, and raised her salary after the very first show. Rita, overnight, became the toast of the Club.

Many were the eager and hungry eyes that surveyed her as she gallivanted about the cabaret floor at the Kitkat giving her best performance just as she had done back at the Avery Burlesque. Being no one's fool, she knew, soon enough, that Vallant in particular was green-eyed with jealousy over her association with Cornell. Vallant would watch her steadily throughout her performance, his intense gaze following every ripple of her supple body, staring into her eyes in the hope of finding some faint display of interest in him on her part.

But jealousy was no cornered commodity as far as Vallant was concerned. Cornell, too, possessed a jealous nature, and his insufferable proprietorship of Rita filled Vallant with agonizing hatred for his boss. Vallant quickly found that Cornell was lavishing gifts — expensive clothes and jewelry — on 'Miss Fox'. He took her to the most expensive nightspots, and frequently had her to dinner or supper at his big country house.

Rita was not unaware of the situation which was developing and purposely did everything to further the tenseness of the atmosphere, even to occasionally looking at Vallant with a vaguely inviting expression on her face — a tantalizing, enigmatic smile which made Vallant tremble with desire for her.

For the first few days the situation remained static. Rita was meanwhile endeavoring to find out how Pat had come to connect herself with these lugs in the first place, and she had made enquiries regarding Stratton.

The newspaper reports from earlier editions of the papers dealing with the drug robbery gave Rita her first clue to the set-up. Some of the vague ideas she had formed from Pat's letters became clearer. Her boyfriend, Stratton, had evidently been working for the chemical firm from which the drugs had been stolen. Knowing that Cornell's organization controlled most of the vice and graft in town, Rita opined that Stratton may have been working for Cornell. The fact that he had disappeared, seemingly without trace, filled Rita with worry. She imagined, at first, that Cornell must have disposed of the boy in order to stem any evidence which Stratton could provide should the cops get the case under control.

Less than a week after her first appearance as the star of the Kitkat cabaret, Cornell was suddenly given a fresh interest to devote his time to. A new outburst of slayings started: the first of the slugged men being the pock-marked Evans, Cornell's own private bodyguard. This was the first time that Molari had struck without some apparent motive. Cornell had no proof that the shooting was done by Molari's mob, but in view of the earlier happenings he was quite content to suspect Molari, and his anger was considerable because Evans had been one of the best trigger-men on the Cornell team. Specially chosen by Cornell, in fact, as one of his lieutenants.

Molari had been building up something of a reputation for himself during the intervening weeks, and already the impact of his 'protection' racket was becoming feared throughout the underworld. Moreover, there was evidence that a number of ex-cons had been pleased to join up with Molari in the hope of rustling some of the proceeds which went into the Cornell coffers. After the shooting of Evans, Cornell lost two more men. One was bumped off right outside the Kitkat early one morning. The other was shot and killed by machine-gun bullets while driving Cornell's car. His steering impaired, he had finished up trying to run the car through a metal fence adjoining the Riverside Garage, and had smashed the vehicle to a pulp, himself inside it.

Several of Cornell's stalwart followers began to exhibit the yellow pennant.

'They're just tryin' to scare us out of existence,' growled Cornell to the assembled deputation that called on him one evening. 'Maybe I was wrong when I figured we should give Molari a bit of rope before fixin' him. I've changed my mind. We're gonna teach that rat a lesson he ain't likely to forget in a hurry.'

The buzz of agreement that followed that declaration left Cornell in no further doubt regarding the feelings of his mobsters.

'Molari's fixed up a headquarters at the Rushton Hotel: he's bought the whole property and plans to reopen the old Rushton Club that used to operate from there during the old prohibition days. It's from that joint that his thugs go out building up their 'protection' round. I've had the joint watched for a couple of weeks and Molari's been followed out to Hope Island, where he's got a hideout at a house back of the beach. Tonight we're goin' out there. I don't want anyone of our lot hurt, understand? — we've lost too many good men already, and the cops would just revel in a shoot-up between the two of us. We've got to make Molari see sense without bringing things to a real showdown. If Molari wants to fight, we'll fight — but that only means wreckin' the whole set-up. What I want to do at the moment is put the fear of Satan into that guy, so's he'll play along for a few more weeks without unleashin' too much lead. I want to leave him alone until he's got this racket of his well sewed-up. That's when we'll *really* take-over, and there'll be a showdown such as that filthy buzzard never dreamed of.'

'What time do we leave?' demanded Podge, eagerly.

'We'll figure that out as soon as we get a report from Freedsom. He's casin' the joint right now.'

'Who's staying here to watch things?' demanded Vallant.

'You are, naturally,' snapped Cornell.

Vallant felt considerably relieved, but didn't show it. He was mighty glad that he'd been left out of the party — there was probably going to be some wild gunning, and Vallant was no armed hero. At the same time it occurred to him that Molari's boys might plan some sort of a retributive onslaught at the Kitkat when they felt the heat of Cornell's mob's slugs. That bothered him enough to force him to ask another question.

73

'You're gonna leave some of the boys here, though, ain't you? Wouldn't do to leave the joint unguarded in case something goes wrong . . . '

Cornell sneered at him.

'I naturally ain't proposin' to leave the joint wide open for wreckin' by Molari's lugs,' he drawled. 'There'll be the usual boys on the door and two more around the back. We'll take two cars — the new one and your Mercury, Vallant. My Packard's just a heap of scrap iron, thanks to Molari. But I'm taking one of his vehicles tonight, just to show him I expect him to show some respect for the guy who runs this town.'

The men in the room were tensed up about their coming fight. They were pretty wild about the shootings of their buddies and glad that Cornell had at last decided to show his hand.

Shortly after that Freedsom put in an appearance with a report on the set-up at the Rushton. His information was enough for Cornell to work on. They decided to take one car to the Rushton and to tail the Molari mob as they left for Hope

Island. The other car, containing seven Cornell guys would wait at the Rushton and check on how many Molari thugs were on the premises. They would then drop off sufficient men to cope with any trouble there, and the rest would follow on to join up with Cornell's first car on the main highway across the bridge to Hope Island. By that time Cornell hoped to have laid a trap for the Molari jalopy and to have ambushed them somewhere in the vicinity of their own hideout.

Molari was not to be killed, if it could be avoided, but the rest of the car-load were to be drilled heavily.

Molari was then to be brought back to the Kitkat for a pep-talk: Cornell intended to talk some sense into him and to warn him about any recurrence of the shootings.

The time fixed was nine o'clock. They might have to hang around the Rushton for three or four hours, but in the meantime a certain amount of checking and reconnoitering could be done. Cornell figured he might be able to think up some plan for wrecking the Rushton headquarters, although he was reluctant to stir up too much trouble at that time in case it led to a real battle of annihilation between the two organizations — a thing to be avoided if possible.

At nine o'clock, to schedule, the two car-loads moved off from the Kitkat, Cornell in the back of the big new Cadillac, with Freedsom driving. Each jalopy carried enough equipment to keep a small battalion going for a week. Cornell was taking no chances.

* * *

Rita Deane, in her role as 'Bubbles' Fox, had two spots to do that night at the Club. Her first act came on at nine-thirty, and the second one at eleven.

For the previous couple of days she had been spending much of her spare time investigating leads which she'd picked up from odd comments made by some of the boys, or from newspaper reports of the drug robbery. She was determined to locate Jimmy Stratton if he was alive, or to find out how he had been disposed of, if Cornell had had him killed. Rita thought that Stratton would have shown up after reading about the death of Pat — her picture had been published in most newspapers and he must have recognized it, even though the cops were still unable to identify her.

The police enquiries among the Cornell crowd had merely established that the young girl had been a friend of Pete Beamish: no one on Cornell's payroll was prepared to offer any further information. They even denied knowing her name. Beamish and Guppy, they said, were the only two who might know anything about her. And Beamish and Guppy the Grid were dead!

Rita finished her first performance. The crowd was thin, since it was still fairly early for the more regular patrons. The later show would be performed to a packed house. She noticed Vallant talking to the two 'bouncers' in the foyer, and something in the atmosphere told her that there was some big business afoot that night, although she heard no whisper of the truth. She thought of asking Vallant, casually, what was happening, but changed her mind and held her curiosity in check. Cornell, she knew, was not on the premises, and he had cancelled their arrangement for supper that night. He was to have taken her to the 'Blue Canary' for a meal between acts. Moreover, she noticed the absence of the lugs who usually drifted in and out of the premises during the night.

The only hint that whatever went on was of a sinister nature came from two of the chorus-girls with whom Rita was passively friendly. Cornell would not permit the fraternization of any of his men with any of the girls in the Club: he was very firm about that rule, and even dismissed girls if they as much as attempted to hand one of his boys a 'come-hither'. Cornell believed in his axiom about women being poison, even though he failed to practice his own dictum where Rita was concerned. But, then, he was the boss, and consequently privileged.

Rita heard the two chorus-cuties

chatting among themselves and realised that despite the strict rule about being friendly with the men, both girls were secretly carrying on with members of Cornell's organization. And from their words Rita learned that the mob was out on a big job that night, with plenty of shooting probable. And that Cornell himself was 'in the saddle' — an unusual thing which denoted the importance of the job.

The opportunity to quiz Vallant seemed to have arrived. Hitherto, because of Cornell's possessiveness, Rita had been unable to do little more than the time of day with Vallant, but she guessed he might prove a valuable source of information, since he had taken over Beamish's job . . .

6

She knew that Vallant had been ogling her all night. The look in his eye was enough to persuade her that she could make him as talkative as she wanted him to be.

She latched the door of her dressing room, and with a faint smile on her lips waited, still in her stage clothes, for the inevitable knock.

'Hello?' she called as the panel vibrated to a firm signal.

'It's me. Vallant. Can I see you a moment?'

'I'm changing,' she called.

'That's okay. I only want to talk.'

'Wait a minute then.'

Still controlling the smile which threatened to break from her lips at the very sight of Vallant's shining eyes she slipped the latch and drew the door open.

He ambled in, languidly, smoking a cigarette. As soon as he was inside he stood with his back to the door and with his hands behind him, latched the lock. She had slipped behind the screen, her head and shoulders alone visible over the top.

'I'm glad you came,' Rita mused. 'I've been wanting to talk to you for a long time. But Cornell's always been around. He's out tonight, isn't he?'

'Maybe he is,' Vallant answered, smoothly. 'I wouldn't know.'

'You'd know all right,' grinned Rita. She climbed out of her stage garb and pulled her kimono around her. Then she came from behind the screen and sat in front of the dressing table, combing her hair. 'There's some sort of a job on, isn't there?' she demanded.

'Maybe,' Vallant said, still uncommunicative. His piercing eyes were ranging over the glossy hair, taking in every admirable feature of her lovely face, reflected in the dusty mirror.

'What did you want to see me about?' Rita asked, still aloofly.

'You've been on my mind,' confessed Vallant. 'For a long time. I guess you know that.'

'I'm Cornell's girl,' she said. 'That should be enough for you.'

'Well it ain't,' he breathed. 'That lug don't mean a thing to you. A girl like you wouldn't take a tumble for such a greasy moron.'

'You're pretty free with your words when he ain't around,' she grinned. 'I'd like to hear you say something like that in his hearing.'

'One of these days I will,' promised Vallant, without much conviction. 'But I don't want to waste time talking about that fat slug. I want to talk about you. About us.'

She half turned on the stool and stared at him.

'About *us?*' she repeated, slowly. 'Just where do you get the idea you can couple yourself to me, mister? I don't even know you.'

'You know me all right. I've watched you every night — every afternoon, for weeks. I've watched you until you must've felt it. And I reckon you've had a yen to talk to me before now — but for Cornell being around all the time.'

'He's a dangerous man,' she muttered. 'I guess he'd get pretty tough if anyone tried anything.'

'He couldn't get tough with us if we weren't here,' said Vallant.

She pretended not to understand his words, although their implication was obvious.

'How'd you mean?'

He grasped her by the shoulders and pulled her to her feet. His arms circled her waist and he drew her close.

She pushed against him, averting her head, and cried: 'Now quit acting like a baboon, Vallant. Someone might come.'

'No one'll come around here just yet,' he said, his voice strangely hoarse with emotion. 'I've waited weeks to get you alone and talk to you. Listen, Babe, you know how I feel. Don't act like this . . .'

She relaxed slightly, permitting him to draw her freely into his embrace. His hot breath was on her hair and she could feel him trembling.

His mouth sought hers, urgently, viciously, and he planted a firm kiss on her lips. She tried again to resist his strength, but found herself grappling with a man of intense passion whose whole mind was aflame with the desire that he'd held under control for so long. His arms increased their pressure and his mouth pressed down on hers until her lips felt bruised and her breathing became difficult.

As she forced herself to relax, fighting for breath, she felt the change that came over the man: his grip became less taut, his emotions less volatile. He held her limply, staring down into her eyes.

'I'm sorry,' he said. 'I guess I've waited too long to do that. You don't know how long . . . '

She drew in great gulps of air, her arms now circling his neck and holding on to him. She felt the gentle pressure of his arm across her back, and then he bent her slightly backwards and kissed her almost tenderly on the eyes and lips.

She had submitted to the embraces and caresses of Cornell reluctantly enough — his gross and repulsive body nauseated her but she suffered it because she was on a mission and intended to fulfil her job at any cost. And she had intended to play with Vallant in the same way — leading him on, taunting and tantalizing him, until he was ready to talk — to tell her all that she wanted to know about Pat and young Stratton and the reason for Pat's association with Beamish. She had been prepared to go to extremes in order to exact the information she wanted. Now her whole mental attitude seemed to be in a state of flux.

His hot kisses on her neck and face seemed to set off emotions within her which she had hitherto held in check.

Her senses were reeling as she said:

'Please. Let me get dressed.' Her voice was a low whisper. Vallant kissed her again. 'It's getting late,' she breathed. 'We can't stay here.'

'I don't want to stay here. I want to take you away. We can go away together. Now. Tonight. Cornell will be busy for a few hours yet. We could be across the border before daybreak. He'd never find you.'

'Gee,' she said, weakly. 'You've got it bad, ain't you?'

'You'll never know. Listen, honey. You like me, don't you? I guess I'm a better bet than that swine Cornell whichever way you look at it. I'd treat you right, honey. Let's get away. Together. Tonight.'

'But . . . '

'Don't stall, honey. You'll never get away from that lug if you hang on here much longer. He's bad — rotten right through. He doesn't even know how to treat a dame. When he's had enough of you, he'll throw you on the scrap-heap like he's thrown dozens of other dames. I'll treat you different, Babe. You wouldn't be takin' any chances. I've got a little dough stacked away. I've been plannin' this for some time now. But we'd have to get clear away — right outa the state. Cornell would turn the country upside down to find us. And he'd kill both of us.'

'Don't I know it,' she answered, releasing herself from his clutch and backing away.

'I want to take care of you,' he said. 'We can go places together. With me you'd amount to something . . . '

The urgent pleading of his voice was

tempered with emotions of uncontrollable desire. She could almost read his thoughts as he gazed at her.

He moved forward again to take her in his arms. She gently pushed him back with her hand. Then she moved across the room and started to snatch at her clothes which were flung across the top of the screen.

'I'd better get some things on,' she said, thinking rapidly. 'We can get away from here and talk. Maybe to the river. Anywhere. It's not safe to hang around here.'

He read partial surrender in her words and his heart felt less heavy.

'You mean you'll come . . . ?'

'We'll talk about it,' she replied, softly. 'But not here. Cornell might get back at any minute. He told me to go straight to the house and wait there until he showed up.'

'You ain't goin'?' Vallant grunted. 'Not back to the house . . . '

'Nope. I guess not. But we've gotta get away from the Club. Someone might talk.'

She was drawing on her stockings, seemingly oblivious to his presence. In her gossamer underclothes the smooth contours of her body glistened in the light. He watched her, fascinated by her bewitching loveliness, his eyes roving over her as he talked:

'Okay. We'll go to my place. Pack whatever things you've got here. I'll get a few things together and we'll hit out for Carolina City. Cornell won't be through till turned midnight — maybe much later.'

She pulled the dress over her head and smoothed it down over her hips. She beckoned him over and asked him to fasten her up.

He took a deep breath and nodded.

He buttoned the back of her dress. She busied herself for a few seconds repairing her make-up. Then she opened the dressing room door and looked out into the corridor. Only the vibration of the orchestra and the rumble of dancing disturbed the silence outside in the passage. She nodded to Vallant and said:

'We'll go out the back way. We'll have

to get a cab. Cornell took the jalopy.'

'Mine too,' Vallant swore. 'I'd forgotten that for the moment. Yeah — we'll have to hop a cab.'

It was as dark as a dungeon in the mews outside. Vallant walked on ahead, swiftly, and reached the main road in a few seconds. There was no traffic on the road and he cursed under his breath.

'We'll pick one up on the corner of Mason Boulevard,' he told Rita. 'Come on. Let's step it out.'

It was five minutes before they managed to hail a passing Redline Cab. Climbing aboard Vallant gave the address of his apartment, adding:

'And step on it, bud. I've got to pack and catch a train.'

★   ★   ★

Rita was in a dilemma. She wanted Vallant to talk. It was her only chance, because Cornell might not take another night off for weeks, and with Cornell around she'd have to toe the line. Having gone so far with the mobster, backing out now would probably mean setting herself in line for a beating-up at least, and probably for a torso full of slugs. She had no doubts about the vicious ruthlessness of Cornell. He had spoken to her plenty, bragging about the number of corpses indirectly and directly attributable to his power in the city.

But at the same time, Rita didn't want to go away with Valliant. That was asking for trouble from two quarters. In the first place it wouldn't take Cornell three seconds to figure out he'd been double-crossed by the pair of them, and in the second place, Vallant was not going to be easy to control once she trusted herself to his guardianship.

Vallant had an apartment in the Untermyer block — a luxury suite of rooms in the elite uptown service apartment block in the city. He led her into the living room and saw her admiring examination of his quarters. Vallant had done himself pretty well. The furnishings and decorations were in good taste, surprisingly and expensive enough to indicate that Vallant's pickings were not peanuts. Whatever else he had against Cornell, he had certainly done well enough for himself out of the organization.

'Come and help me pack, honey,' Vallant invited after they had sampled his liquor. 'I won't be long.'

Her eyes strayed towards the adjoining room. His bedroom. She blew out a thin stream of smoke. A guy wanting to pack a few hasty pieces of luggage for an out-of-town emergency hop didn't need any help. She read his insinuation and stalled.

'We could stay here for a while,' she offered. 'Cornell wouldn't figure on us being together and it'd be several hours before he tumbled to what's happened. I thought you wanted to talk to me?'

'I do.'

'Well, I want to talk to you, too,' she commented. 'About Cornell, and one or two other things. I want to get a few things straightened out. I'm fairly new to this set-up you know.'

'Sure,' he acknowledged, frowning. 'But that don't matter no more. We're quittin'.

We're gettin' away . . . '

'Some things still puzzle me,' she remarked, walking towards the window and standing there, looking at him. 'I thought maybe you'd wise me up about 'em.'

'Sure I will, honey. All in good time. We'll have lots of time to talk about the past. We're gonna be together for a long time, ain't we . . . ?' He paused. 'We can talk while I'm packin'. C'mon and lend a hand.'

She sighed. He was walking into the bedroom. She followed, slowly, still smoking and drawing deeply on the cigarette. She stood in the doorway and watched him as he hauled a leather valise from beneath the bed and thrust it, open, upon the bureau. Then he started to rummage in the drawers of his tallboy, dragging out shirts, collars and under-wear. He threw an armful of garments haphazardly into the bag.

'How long've you been with Cornell?' asked Rita.

'Now listen, 'Bubbles',' groaned Val-lant, 'quit botherin' about that right now. We've got to get out of here first. There'll be plenty of time to talk. C'mon over here and bring your bag in. I can pack most of your things into this valise, then we'll only have the one piece to lug around.'

'Okay,' she muttered, biting her lower lip. 'I'll get it.'

She retraced her steps and returned shortly with her small week-end case in which she kept a few things at the Club. She threw it on to the floor. Her mind was fathoming the problem of getting Vallant to talk. She wanted to find out as much as she could without having to go with him. Once she quit the Club, Cornell would be on her tail like a ton of bricks: her chances of finding anything out would be gone.

She said: 'What kind of a guy was Beamish?'

He stopped packing and looked at her.

'Pete Beamish?' His eyes bored into hers. 'What d'you want to know about *him* for?'

'He was your boss wasn't he? Before he got killed?'

'How did you know he got killed?'

'Cornell mentioned something about it.

Casually. It got me interested.'

'He was okay,' shrugged Vallant. 'Quite a brainy guy. I liked him, I guess. But you know the way things go.'

'No I don't. Why was he killed? I heard he was mixed up with some woman.'

'Yeah, that's right.'

'Is that why Cornell killed him? Was she Cornell's girl?'

'No, of course not. She was just a dame. A kid. Worked at the Club for a while. Not long.'

'Was Beamish keen on her?'

Vallant straightened up and moved across to her.

'Listen, honey,' he said. 'There's not time for all these damn fool questions. Just forget all about this mob. Forget it. We'll be out of it soon.'

'But I want to know,' she insisted. 'It puzzles me.'

'You're a queer dame, sometimes,' he growled. 'What's it matter? Beamish got tied up with the dame, that's all. He took her across to the Island. Some other bunch of lugs moved in an' shot 'em up. Three of 'em.'

'Why?'

'I don't know why,' he stormed. 'I guess they were kinda sore with Beamish, or maybe with Cornell.'

'Tell me about it,' she pleaded. 'It'll help me to understand Cornell. He's out on some job tonight. Is that connected with the shooting of Beamish and — and the others?'

'Well, yeah, in a way,' he admitted.

'Who had Cornell gone gunnin' for?'

'Oh, just some lout from out of town.'

'Y'mean he knows who was responsible for Beamish's death?'

'There's an even chance he knows the guy who was responsible.'

Vallant was studying her face. There was something there that worried him.

'Listen, 'Bubbles,' what makes you so damned interested in Beamish?' he demanded. 'You ain't askin' all these damn fool questions for nothin'. What goes on?'

She smiled. 'I told you. I'm just interested to get a sort of background to the set-up. I never realized I was letting myself in for anything like this. I just figured I'd have a job in the Club — like I wanted. I never realized Cornell was the kind of guy he is. I never knew I'd be movin' into an organization like this.'

'Maybe it's as well you don't know too much,' mumbled Vallant. 'Sometimes it's dangerous to know too much. Cornell is the biggest racketeer in town. He controls almost every dive in the place, and his mob is the most crooked and diabolical assembly of louts that ever was. To tell you the truth I ain't sorry to be runnin' out on this bunch, honey. A guy's life ain't never safe.'

'You mean you were figurin' on takin' a powder before you met me?'

'Maybe I was. But now it makes it all the more important to steer away. So let's not waste any more time, honey. We c'n talk about the past when we're in the clear.'

She clutched his arm and looked up into his face. Her becoming smile fastened itself on his eyes.

'We're safe enough here for a while, ain't we? You don't want me to have all these questions on my mind, do you? I'd feel so much more easy in my mind if I knew what was going on. Why don't you tell me, Bruce?'

It was the first time she'd used his name. The look in her eyes did things to his bloodstream. His arms reached out and drew her close against him.

'Sure I'll tell you everythin' honey, but why don't you be reasonable an' wait? Let's get in the clear, for Pete's sake.'

'No. I want to know now. It's worryin' me.'

He shrugged, and leaning towards her, kissed her.

'I want to know about the woman Beamish was with,' Rita said, softly. 'How did she come to get mixed up with this mob in the first place?'

Bruce Vallant sighed heavily. He stole a look at his watch: it was getting on for midnight. He thought of the outfit moving in towards Molari's hideout. God alone knew what was going on out there, and Vallant was glad enough to have been spared the operation. Cornell would find out quickly enough how he'd been double-crossed during his absence, and there was no going back now. Vallant had only one thought in his mind — to put as much distance between Cornell and himself as possible, and to take Bubbles Fox with him.

Her nearness was destroying him. He could feel the gentle pressure of her warm body against his and the fragrance of the scent of her hair. He kissed her fiercely, almost biting her lips.

'Bruce. Not now,' said Rita. 'Let's get the talk straightened out first . . . You were telling me about Beamish . . . '

Suddenly Vallant picked her up. She looked into his eyes and for a moment felt the surge of apprehension rising inside her. He carried her over to the bed and threw her down upon the soft covers

'Bruce, not here . . . ' she said, trembling. 'Why can't you be reasonable? Tell me what I want to know . . . '

'I don't feel like talkin'. I never felt less like talkin' in my life,' he muttered.

The next moment Rita felt the cold sensation of acute horror as a wave of air entered the stuffy room and the sound of noisy footsteps and banging pierced the celestial silence. A loud clatter, coming nearer, emanated from the living room. Almost without notice, the door of the bedroom had been flung open and she heard someone call:

'Vallant. Are you there? Where . . . ?' Then the voice stopped. A low, hoarse cry ended the inquiry. Then booming more terrifyingly came the rapped expression:

'Well, for Pete's sake . . . So *this* is what's been goin' on, eh?' The menacing malice of the words cut through the atmosphere: never had Rita felt the impact of such venom in a few mean words.

Vallant had jerked himself to his feet and was standing — quivering almost — beside the bed, staring in horror at the man in the doorway. His face was ashen and beads of sweat formed miraculously on his forehead.

Cornell stood in the doorway, an extremely hideous sight. His clothes were grimy and disheveled, his face smothered with mud and blood. There was blood upon his suit, and on his collar. His necktie was askew, one flap of the collar digging into a mass of blood on the neck-band of his jacket.

In his hand, also bloody and begrimed, he held a large Luger. Rita screamed — reaction from the confusion of emotions. She tried to haul herself off the bed but Cornell's curt and vicious hissing held her motionless, petrified:

'Stay right where you are, you bitch. And you, too, Mister Vallant.'

Cornell moved into the room, closing the door behind him without turning.

Vallant squealed hoarsely:

'You — you've been hurt, boss . . . '

Cornell snorted: 'Yeah. That's right. Hurt. I got a slug in my shoulder but it's not deep.'

He stared from the trembling, unsteady figure of Vallant whose bloodshot eyes were rolling with fear, to the girl lying apprehensively on the bed. His voice was coldly menacing, low and controlled.

'We met with trouble. Molari's mob is bigger than I figured — and someone had tipped the swine off. We've got a four-flusher or two in the outfit, Vallant. In fact the whole ruddy set-up seems t'be littered with four-flushers. You seem to have been havin' quite a time here, you two, huh?' His ugly, contorted face leered closer to Vallant.

'Looks like it was Fate brought me here, not this slug in my shoulder. Y'see, Vallant, I rang the Club awhile back. I wanted you to bring a car out to the Island but they said you couldn't be located. So I figured maybe you were plannin' to come out an' lend a hand. I didn't reckon you'd be double-dealin' this way, Mister Vallant. I hardly expected you to have the guts to try an' take my dame.

'An' I see you've been stickin' a few things in your overnight bag. Seems like you might have been plannin' to take a trip. Ah — an' Bubbles, too, I see. You also packed a few dainties, did ya? How very delicate of you!' His voice was getting rougher, the hand holding the gun trembling more and more. The hatred in his expression was demoniacal. 'Well, Vallant, it's a pity you didn't get started earlier. You ain't gonna have the chance to take my dame away, now. I may have been hit, but I ain't paralyzed. There's two slugs left in this shooter, and they're reserved for you, you skulkin', yellow-bellied rat. First you was too scared to come out on the job with the boys, an' while I'm tied up protectin' your interests as well as my own, you steal off with my dame an' try to take her! That wasn't a very clever move Mister Vallant. You should've had more patience. I might 'ave gotten tired of 'Bubbles' here in a few weeks and then you could have had her without all this bother . . . '

'You can't do this, Cornell!' Vallant gasped. 'I couldn't help it . . . the dame gave me the come-on. She made me . . . '

Rita stared at him aghast. His face had gone green and his whole body was quivering with funk.

Cornell snapped: 'That's the way, you louse. Blame anyone, except yourself. You miserable skunk. You needn't blame the floosie. I know how it is. She done the same to me . . . It's no good hollerin' about it, Vallant. You're gettin' yours, and you're gettin' it right now . . . '

Cornell's face twisted itself into a mask

of utter fury. He fired, coldly, malevolently, without altering the expression on his face. The bullet hit Vallant somewhere in the chest, and a gasp of pain was flung from his lips as he staggered forward.

Cornell grinned savagely, and pulled the trigger again.

The second slug bit deep into Vallant's face, somewhere near his right eye. His face became a mass of blood as with a shriek of terror he staggered and fell forward, clutching the floor with his fingers. His body shuddered and writhed on the carpet. Rita let out a long piercing shriek. Cornell snapped:

'Close your damned mouth or I'll close it for you now instead of later. I'm gonna teach you a lesson before you go the same way as this rat . . . '

He bounded forward, thrusting the gun into his pocket. Rita tried to scramble out of his way, but his lumbering, bloodied figure was upon her before she could escape.

Despite his warnings she could no longer restrain her voice and a loud shriek came from her lips. He fell over her across the bed, pinning her shaking body to the covers. One of his hands stole up and fastened firmly across her mouth, forbidding further noise.

He was breathing savagely, his body thrust against hers. She could scarcely breathe or move . . . Then oblivion stole across her and she almost wept with relief to find that unconsciousness gripped her in its protective clutch like some invisible ally . . . Her last memory of that horrible night was the glazed and searing look in Cornell's dreadful eyes as she blinked at him before succumbing to the darkness of the coma.

7

Rita awoke with a start, as though releasing herself from some frantic and oppressing nightmare. Her eyes were heavy-lidded and almost glued together with the white gum of dried, sleepy tears. Her lips trembled as she slowly forced her eyes open, lifting one of her hands and rubbing away the film that fastened the lids down. Her whole body ached with pain, as though she was bruised from head to toe.

For a moment she could remember nothing, and then slowly the full dread of the experience overwhelmed her and she started to weep and shake, biting her bruised lips.

'Take it easy, Miss,' someone said. A cold shiver passed through her body, leaving her with a feeling that her spine was made of ice.

She forced her lips open and sucked in air. Then she opened her eyes and, fearfully, pulled herself up and looked around her.

She was in bed.

In a strange room.

The covers around her were cool and satiny. As her eyes became accustomed to the light, she peered across the void that confronted her and gradually through the blurred vision a few details impinged themselves on her brain. It was a small room, with an open window facing her, through which cool morning air drifted, raising the flimsy curtains in a gentle flurry. The bed was a small one, single-sized, with low panels at the foot. Beside the bed stood a small table on which there reposed a lamp and some books and a glass. In one corner of the room was a tall-boy, and in another, a large wardrobe. Beneath the window was a writing-table bearing a lamp, a type-writer, and some other objects she could not clearly make out.

There was a fire-grate on one wall, but the grate was empty, and on the hearth stood a portable electric fire, its radiants agleam.

Then she was aware of the man standing beside her. He was a youngish man, tall and lanky. He was staring down at her, stroking his chin thoughtfully. She noticed that in his hand he still held the cup of coffee. Now she seemed to have some recollection of warm coffee being forced between her lips. That was what had awakened her.

'You'll feel okay soon,' said the voice again. 'Just take it easy and don't be scared no more.'

She felt the deep solace ingrained in his words and with an effort threw off the returning apprehension that fought to overwhelm her again. As she relaxed, she looked down at the covers of the bed and noticed that they were stained with blood in places. The memory of the night before — for she imagined it must be only one night ago since her dreadful experience — became more clear. The blood awakened the fullest recollection of her struggle with the enraged and brutal mobster.

'How did I — How did I . . . ?' she said weakly.

'How did you get here? I brought you here. Drink this, miss. You'll feel better when you get something warm down your pipes.'

She took the cup with trembling hands and felt grateful to the man for not leaving her to cope with it herself. She hadn't the strength to hold it. He tilted it so that she could gulp down some of the contents.

'There's a dram or two of bourbon in it. I thought it might help things along,' said the stranger.

'I could use a spot of the stuff neat,' she said, faintly.

'Okay. I thought maybe you couldn't stomach it, but here it is,' he answered. He handed her a tumbler containing three or four fingers of brandy.

This time she grasped the glass firmly and swigged off the entire contents.

'Well, it's good medicine if you can hold it,' grinned the stranger.

As the liquor burned its way into her stomach she felt her strength returning. She hoisted herself upright, leaning back against the pillow. Then she noticed she was wearing pajamas. Big, loose pajamas. A man's sleeping-suit. Her face started to color as she said:

'You didn't tell me how I got here . . . '

'I did,' he said. 'I told you I brought you here.'

'Who . . . who . . . where is this place?'

'You're quite safe here for the time being. It's a small apartment in Chinatown. The back of beyond. No one would ever find you here. I've used it myself as a hide-out for months.'

'But — but I was.'

'I know. You were at Vallant's apartment and you're wondering how you managed to get away. Well don't bother your noodle about it for the moment because you're pretty sick, kid, and you need a little rest. I washed most of the blood off you, but I couldn't cope with it all. I'll leave you to clean yourself up a little and straighten yourself out. Your duds are on the floor in a valise. I repacked them for you.'

She frowned.

'Say,' she murmured. 'I must be dreaming. I was at Vallant's place last night . . . and . . . Cornell showed up. He shot Vallant and . . . and . . . ' She paused. 'I've got that much right, ain't I?'

He nodded. 'Sure. That's right. Cornell slugged Vallant. Two shots. One between the eyes and one in the ribs.'

'How . . . how did I get into these — pajamas?'

'I'm afraid I had to fix you up with 'em,' returned the young man. 'You were — well — pretty much in need of something when I found you.'

'When? Where?' she demanded, curiously.

'Listen, kid,' he said — she felt curiously amused by his use of the word kid, since she figured she was a year or two older than he was — 'we'll talk about it as soon as you feel more yourself. I've got to slip away for an hour. Something I have to do. You'll be okay here for a while. I didn't get much sleep myself last night — had to doss down on the floor in the living room, so I feel a little sour myself. I'm goin' to slip down an' freshen up at the gym, around the corner. Si Lung Fi's place — but you wouldn't know it. I'll be back as soon as soon. Meanwhile, you clean yourself up a trifle an' make yourself at home.'

'What time is it?'

'Around eight, I guess.'

'Are — you — are you the only one livin' here?'

'Yeah. That's right.'

'It's all very odd,' she commented, wonderingly.

'It'll explain itself in time,' he assured her.

'But who *are* you?' she demanded.

'*Nemesis*,' he drawled, with an odd expression on his face.

'Who?' she repeated, perplexed.

'Nemesis. Maybe you wouldn't understand. Nemesis is a guy with a chip on his shoulder. A guy with a job to do. A guy who's out to get himself a slice of revenge, see? I'll tell you somethin' about it when I get back. You do as I say and get yourself presentable. An' don't leave here. It wouldn't be safe yet awhile.'

'Oh. Is . . . ?'

'I'm breezin' now,' he told her. 'Be back shortly. Remember — keep the door closed and don't let anyone in. You'll recognize my voice when I get back. I'll holler through the grill.'

He walked towards the door. There, he paused and stared at her. 'Y'know,' he said, strangely, 'you remind me of someone. It's queer. But you've got the exact look she had . . . '

'Who?'

'A girl. A girl I — My girl.'

'Your girl?' Rita felt suddenly amused. 'Say, you're goin' to have a heck of a time explainin' this away ain't you — I mean if she should show up . . . ?'

His voice was strained.

'She won't show up. She's dead,' he said, quietly.

Rita stared at him. She watched his face, saw the twitching of the muscles of his jaw. He was dressed in a dark lounge suit, rather crumpled. His beard was noticeably stubbly. Otherwise he was quite presentable, good-looking and nicely-made, even if not bulky. Abruptly a swift thought assailed her. She muttered, gently:

'You don't mean — Pat? You ain't Stratton are you?'

His eyes creased and the frown at his forehead deepened.

'Pat? How come you know about Pat? And how did you guess my name?'

Rita drew in a deep breath. 'You *are* Stratton! Now it begins to add up a little. But why . . . '

He was across the room. Savagely he gripped her arms and stared into her face.

'Say, who the deuce are you?' he snapped. 'I knew you as 'Bubbles' Fox — Betty Fox. I heard about you. But there's something more to it than that? You couldn't have known about Pat — nor me . . . What's the game . . . ?'

'It's no game,' she said, her eyes misting up. 'I'm Rita. Rita Deane. Pat's sister.'

He released her as though he'd been stung.

'Rita? The sister Pat told me about? But for Pete's sake, how did you horn yourself into this set-up . . . ? I thought you were playing Burlesque . . . miles away? Pat said . . . '

She got out of bed. Across the rail was a coat — his coat. She put it on, and then sat down on the edge of the bed.

'We've both got a lot of explainin' to do,' she observed. 'But I feel a damn sight better now that I know who you are. I've been tryin' to locate you for a long time. I don't quite see how you found me or why you brought me here from Vallant's apartment. I feel as sore as hell and as confused as the devil, but that'll pass, I guess. The main thing is that now I've got a chance to even things up. I wanted to find you so's I could get the truth. I didn't understand how Pat came to be with that mob. Why she was with Beamish the night they shot Beamish up . . . '

'Listen, kid,' Stratton exclaimed: 'Let's get cleaned up and go someplace where we can figure things out. I've got to get you out of here as soon as possible because Cornell'll tear the city apart tryin' to find you. There's an old jalopy down the road, belongs to a Chinese pal of mine. I c'n borrow that an' we can hit out for the Island and hide out there for a couple of days. I guess the best thing we can do is get started right away. We can get some food on the way. How's about that?'

114

'Anythin' you say, Jimmy,' she said, earnestly. 'I just want to get to the bottom of all this, that's all. An' I want to find the guy who shot Pat. That's what I want to do — find the guy. I'm gonna make him wish he'd . . . '

Stratton took her wrist and pulled her off the bed.

'Lay off that, kid,' he snapped. 'That's my job. That's what I've been workin' on for weeks. You get yourself ready for the trip. You don't have to bother your head about the guy who — plugged Pat. He's my pigeon.'

She stared at his face and saw the glint in his eye and the firm set of his jaw. There was no mistaking the violent fury that lay behind those clear, menacing eyes. Whoever had been responsible for Pat Dean's sudden death had plenty of trouble coming to him.

* * *

They drove out along the highway, the two cases piled in the boot, the old jalopy clanking away as though it would fall to pieces if they struck any rough roads.

He explained how he had got mixed up with the Cornell mob. About the money he'd owed to Cornell and how Cornell had forced him to do the dirty on his firm by stealing the drugs that the mob wanted for shipment abroad.

Then, with the cops trailing him, Stratton had had to hide out, and he had found the small apartment in Chinatown, owned by a friend of his who ran a small laundry. The place was off the beaten track, and there were plenty of Chinese friends of Si Lung Fi who would tip off Stratton if anything suspicious threatened him. He hadn't been able to contact Pat — mainly because he didn't want *her* drawn into the trouble with any cops. His idea was to find a way of forcing Cornell into a corner so that he'd have evidence that he had been forced to do the job. The trouble was that Cornell had the cops tied up and helpless. They were as scared of Cornell as hell. The whole city was in the grip of Cornell's outfit, and the law was more or less impotent against the top guys of the organization. They pulled in some of the lesser lights now and again, but there was so little direct evidence against the Big Shots that the cops were sick and tired of the name of Cornell and the few top-ranking lieutenants who worked with him. Their main hope, now that gang warfare was once again showing signs of revival, was that some other outfit would put paid to Cornell's empire.

Stratton had managed to keep tabs on the Cornell outfit for some time without showing himself. He knew that Woolf Cornell was anxious to find him, as well as the cops, because Cornell was afraid of Stratton's inside knowledge of the organization. If Stratton could find out where the shipment had gone, the cops would be able to trace back right to the Cornell doorstep, and there was plenty of evidence of illicit dope-peddling to be picked up in a certain quarter of the city. Cornell had not been too anxious to traffic in dope: it was one of his former lieutenants (now killed by Cornell's personal bodyguard) who had started that side of the business. Cornell had found himself in too deep to back out and had

had to pursue the commitments already planned.

While Stratton had been figuring out a plan of action and worrying about Pat, he had learned of the shooting on the highway from Hope Island in which Beamish, Pat and Guppy had been slaughtered. That was the first he had known about Pat's interference in the game. He had not expected her to take a chance like she had done. Now, he realized that Pat had deliberately wormed her way into the organization with the intention of doing, more quickly, what he himself had wanted to do. She had intended to get the evidence — the strong vital evidence — against Cornell, on which the cops would be able to work. At the same time, the information would help to minimize Stratton's sentence when his case came up.

Clearly it had been Pat's intention to get such evidence and to make Stratton turn himself over to the cops and take his chance. She loved him so much that she didn't want him to be an outlaw for the rest of his life, dodging the cops and living on his wits and nerves for the rest of his days.

'That would be like Pat,' said Rita, misty-eyed. 'She was a lovely kid. I guess it was as much my fault as anyone's. I was supposed to be takin' care of her. But she wrote me often an' told me about you — said she was going along okay and that you an' her were goin' to get married soon . . .'

Jim Stratton nodded savagely: 'Yeah. That's the way it was. Until I messed things up.'

'It wasn't your fault,' Rita consoled him.

'Sure it was my fault,' he retorted, angry with himself. 'I had no right to get into Cornell's hands like I did. I wanted some dough, quickly, so's Pat an' me could get married. I was only earnin' peanuts with the firm I worked for, an' I couldn't have got married on that — not to have given Pat a straight deal. So I started visitin' the gamin' hall back of the Kitkat. There's a fine set-up, back there — everythin, from Bacarat to Chemy and Roulette — dice an' everythin'. An' like the sap I was, I never cottoned on to the fact that they were deliberately lettin' me win at first. The whole set-up is crooked — the tables faked, the dice loaded — even the liquor there is phoney hooch. I won a few dollars — a few hundred dollars. I was on Easy Street, I thought. One last flutter just to get my nest egg lookin' sizable enough to ask Pat to marry me right away . . . one last fling. I took my roll along there and played the tables all night. Couldn't do a thing right. Y'know how it gets you — you find yourself so deep in, you can't let up. I didn't let up. Cornell's thugs were watchin' me all night. I got down to my last dollar, and then someone slipped me a stack of chips and said they was with Cornell's compliments. I played 'em, hopin' I'd get myself out of the red. I lost the lot. Two hundred dollars' worth. I was leavin' the table when some guy came up to me an' said Cornell wanted to see me. They forced me to go to his office. He acted kind of friendly. Said I could play on if I liked — that my credit was good with him because I had played there for a few days. He talked me into it. Talked me into signin' a paper for another five hundred bucks — givin' me a present of the two hundred I'd already lost. Well — it was the same story. I thought maybe with the five hundred I could win back the losings, and also earn a few dollars extra. But I lost. Lost the lot. Found myself owing Cornell five c's — and me with a weekly paycheck of forty-five dollars. I thought of Pat. I was worried sick. Y'know how it is when you get in a spot like that . . . '

Rita nodded sympathetically. He was just a young kid. Cornell had him all wrapped up. It had been a cinch. He continued with his story, driving automatically, watching the road ahead almost absently:

'Well, that was when they put the pressure on. Cornell knew about a consignment of drugs leavin' the warehouse that weekend. He knew that I was sufficiently trusted by the company to have access to the whole works. He made me arrange for the consignment to be hi-jacked. They took every ounce of stuff on board, hurried it to the dock and shipped it the same night.

'I didn't have much of a chance. I knew Cornell would make me pay pretty dearly over that debt — I would have lost my job in any case, but Cornell wouldn't have stopped there. If I'd refused to do what he wanted, they'd have worked me over good and proper. So that was that. I was stuck with a one-way proposition. I had to take it on the lam. Every cop in town was lookin' for me. They went through my apartment — a small place I had near the factory — with a comb. They watched the joint night and day. I couldn't even get in to grab my clothes an' things. I hightailed it out to Chinatown and looked up Si Lung. He was a pal of mine from the days when I was a news-kid in that district. He fixed things for me to hide out there, and even had some of his boys keep tabs on Cornell and the cops. But I still couldn't contact Pat because I was scared in case they were tailin' her or listenin' on on her 'phone calls. The next thing I knew was when I read in the papers about the shootin'. For a while I was knocked all of a heap an' couldn't fathom it out. Then I cottoned onto the truth. Pat had deliberately tried to find the evidence I needed to clear myself and to fix Cornell good and certain, once and for all. Unfortunately the kid didn't have much of a chance. She ran into that trouble with the other mob, and got killed . . . '

Rita was crying gently again. Stratton took a deep breath, and hurling his hand into his pocket drew out a package of cigarettes and a lighter.

'Light me one, too,' he commanded, more intent upon stopping her crying, than smoking.

She lighted the two cigarettes and passed one across the wheel to Jim. For a few moments they drove on in silence, each with thoughts of their own.

Abruptly Rita said: 'How about last night, though?'

'Oh, that? Well, I'd been keepin' an eye on the mob as I told you. The China boy had some of his guys out keepin' tabs for me, as well. I'd heard about you joinin' the Kitkat, and I also knew that Bruce

Vallant had taken over from Beamish. I figured that maybe Vallant, being Beamish's successor, could tell me something about the things I wanted to know — about Pat, about the shootin' over on Hope Island, an' all that. Then I picked up the information that Cornell and a fair sized posse of his guys were aimin' to clean out a nest of opposition which had started up in town over at the Rushton. I figured it gave me a good chance to get a closer look into things, 'cos it was certain that a number of Cornell's guys would be occupied elsewhere last night. So I hung around the Club, waitin' a chance to grab hold of Vallant. I heard from Si Lung's contact guy that Vallant would be controllin' things at the Club durin' the shoot-out.

'Well, Vallant wasn't one of the guys I'd come into direct contact with before — when Beamish was handling things at the Club, Vallant was one of Cornell's lieutenants operating from his house out of town — Vallant was a big-time racketeer himself in San Francisco until a year or so back, you know? I hadn't quite worked out my scheme, but I'd planned out tryin' to get him to double-cross Cornell somehow. Thought maybe that if I proved to Vallant that I could get Cornell twenty years, or even the hot-seat, with sufficient evidence, the rat might see a way to getting complete control of Cornell's organization for himself — so's he'd be a Big Shot like he was back in 'Frisco.

'I managed to get into his office — and he never showed up. Lookin' through the window later I saw you an' Vallant leavin' by the back way, an' I figured maybe you were double-crossin' Cornell — for I knew you were Cornell's dame — or at least, that was the idea going around the town.

'I tailed you to Vallant's apartment — I knew where it was anyway. I just couldn't figure out a way to get hold of the guy, then. It was obvious that he was plannin' to run out on Cornell anyway, an' that sort of mussed up my original scheme. I hung around the apartment, lookin' for Vallant's jalopy, thinkin' maybe it would be a good idea to hide away in the car an' be taken wherever it was you and Vallant were headin'. I couldn't find the jalopy. No sign of it.

'Then I saw the disturbance coming off — the sudden appearance of Cornell, looking like a blood-bathed porpoise. I felt it was time to blow. I couldn't see how Vallant could get away before Cornell bounced in, and there was no way of tipping him off about Cornell's return. I didn't see why Vallant had been so long: if he'd only pulled into his apartment to get his things packed into a valise, he was taking a hell of a time about it. Then I remembered you were with him, and of course I didn't know you were not just a gun moll — I had no reason to think anything about you at all, except that you and Vallant were pullin' out an' double-crossin' Cornell.

'I breezed off an' took a cab back to the apartment in Chinatown. But I couldn't sleep. Something was botherin' me an' I wanted to find out what had happened at Vallant's apartment. If Vallant was still alive, there was a chance yet that I could get the information I wanted — maybe more so now.

'So I trailed back to the apartment. It was early in the morning — around one or two. Quiet as hell.

'The rest you can guess. I made for Vallant's quarters and there was no sign of activity. I sneaked in and took a look around. Vallant was as cold as a piece of pork, stretched out on the floor. You were unconscious on the bed . . . Not a pretty sight at all. Cornell had left you just as you were — I covered you up with a blanket and then realized that you were in a tough position if the cops showed up. I hadn't any reason for feeling sorry for you, really, but I guess I did. Cornell had evidently scooted off to get some of his jerks along to take Vallant out of the way and dump the body in the river, or somewhere. He evidently imagined that no one would show up for an hour or two and that he'd have time to get the apartment cleaned up. He never thought you'd have the inclination or the life left to take a powder, even if you came to. So I took you out of the apartment, down the back stairs and dumped you in a corner of the mews while I went and brought Si Lung's old jalopy around the back and hoisted you on board.

'I'd only driven half a mile when I saw Cornell and three of his mobsters pass me on the highway, heading back to Vallant's apartment.

'The rest is as you know it: you were cold and unconscious and in a hell of a mess. I cleaned you up as best I could — gave you a rub down and tucked you into bed. I felt all-in myself by then, so I dossed down on the floor. And that's all there is to it . . . except that I just ain't sure of your reasons for hanging around the Cornell mob. I suppose you had some idea of doin' much the same as Pat was doin' — ? You wanted to find out why Pat had been shot? Where she figured in the set-up?'

Rita nodded.

'Yes. I saw the report in the paper while I was playing at the Avery Burlesque. I made straight for town and palmed myself off as 'Bubbles' Fox. Vallant wouldn't hire me without gettin' Cornell's okay. That's how I came to be interviewed by the big louse himself. He took a liking to me. I knew I'd got to play it that way. I had a notion maybe Cornell was to blame for Pat's death — that he might have deliberately had Beamish and that other mobster bumped off for reasons of his own. I wasn't sure. I had to find out for myself. There was only one way — that was to play ball with Cornell — the wicked swine. You don't know just what a rotten buzzard that rat is, Jimmy.'

He looked at her strangely.

'You certainly took a lot of punishment kid,' he said. 'It must've been pretty dreadful bein' with Cornell, when you hated his guts so much?'

'It was,' she breathed. 'But there was nothing else for it. I didn't even know where you figured in the business, and more than anything else, except finding who killed Pat, I wanted to know where you'd got to, and why Pat was havin' anythin' to do with that mob in the first place.'

They were driving across the wide

bridge now, heading due east. Jimmy said: 'We won't be long now. I reckon we ought to be fairly safe over on the east side of the island. There's a nook called Franciston Bay there — I know the guy who runs the hotel. We can hide out there until we know what's what. I'm curious to know what went wrong with Cornell's scheme last night.'

'Do you know the outfit he was gunnin' for?' she demanded.

'Yeah. I do now,' he replied. 'There's a guy named Molari in town. Newcomer, from Chicago. He had quite a lot of luck in the Midwest but the cops finally made things too hot for him. He hot-footed it to the coast, havin' heard about the big pickin's around this part of the world. Then he came up against Cornell everywhere he went. He hadn't figured on Cornell controllin' every vice in the city — every gamblin' hall, every saloon, every nightspot, all the liquor trafficking and now the dope traffic. I guess it must have given Molari a sort of inferiority complex. For the past few weeks he's been tryin' to scare Cornell into retirement. Wants to muscle in on Cornell's empire, I guess. Cornell ain't the kind of guy to sit home playin' gin-rummy while some outsider beats his gums all over town tellin' the underworld that Cornell's had his day and that the Great Molari from Chicago is hornin' in. So that's what Cornell has in his bonnet, y'see. He an' Molari don't see eye to eye an' Cornell is gettin' tired of Molari's interference. The cops, meanwhile, are probably waitin' for the two louts to meet up for one big shoot-out that'll exterminate both outfits. Then the cops can move in, fairly safely, and clean up the mess. But neither Cornell not Molari wants that situation to arise — which is the reason Cornell was playing a waiting game. He waited too long. Molari was snipin' too many of Cornell's good men. So Cornell decided to have a show-down last night. Something went wrong. Cornell seems to have taken a beatin'. I'd like to know more about that.'

'Me too.' said Rita, thoughtfully. 'An' do you reckon Molari was responsible for the killin' of Beamish and Guppy — and — and Pat?'

'It's probably the way it was,' Jimmy nodded grimly. 'I guess it could have happened that way. Maybe Molari did it to show Cornell his strength.'

Rita stammered: 'You mean — d'you mean that he'd cold-bloodedly kill three people just as a warning to Cornell?'

Jimmy said, quietly: 'Rita, you don't seem to realize what these fiends are capable of. They stop at nothin'. *Nothin'*. It wouldn't mean a thing to either of 'em to bump off three members of an opposition outfit.'

'But — but Pat wasn't a member . . . she wasn't . . . '

Jimmy shook his head.

'That won't make any difference to these lugs. And anyway, Molari wasn't to know Pat wasn't a member of Cornell's outfit. She was evidently passing herself off as Beamish's girl. The foolish little idiot . . . '

'I'm sorry, Jimmy. I guess — I guess you were fond of her. More so than I was, maybe . . . '

Jimmy didn't answer for a moment. His mouth was set in a thin line and his eyes were straying up and down the road ahead.

'We'll get even with the swines,' he muttered, eventually. 'We'll find a way to get even . . .'

'Jimmy,' Rita whispered, 'what would happen to you if the cops caught up with you?'

'I'd maybe get five years. It's a Federal offence.'

'But you could put up a fair enough case . . . you were almost bludgeoned into doin' it. The cops know the strength. They know just how tough Cornell can get . . .'

'Yeah,' said Jimmy bitterly. 'They're scared of him. Scared of the guy. You can't fight ruthless gunmen with the thin stuff of the law. There's only one way to wipe out these thugs and that's to arm the cops, and to shoot first and ask for names and addresses afterwards. But the cops can't operate that way. They're hamstrung with their own darned regulations.

'When they get hold of guys like me, who're indirectly linked to the mob, they do their damnedest to get a strong sentence. It looks good with the public, y'see, and the cops know that Cornell wouldn't be bothered a great deal about me takin' a stiff rap. Nothin' can get away from the fact that I caused that stuff to be hi-jacked. The law'll say that I ought to have turned stool-pigeon. I'll take a rap because of it. The law wouldn't want to know that if I hadn't gone through with it, Cornell would have shot my lungs out, and dumped me in the river strapped to a granite slab.'

After a moment Rita acknowledged what he said.

'You're right, Jimmy. So that puts you back where you started. We've got to find a way of gettin' the evidence we want.'

'It ain't your job,' he reminded her. 'Pat's gone now. There's nothin' more for me to bother about except clearin' myself with the State. I ain't got much to live for — I only had Pat. She was all I had, all I wanted. That was how I came to get into this mess in the first place — wantin' her so bad.'

'I understand, Jimmy,' Rita said softly, laying her hand on his arm. 'An' it's still my affair as much as yours, Jimmy. I won't rest until the guy who killed Pat is as cold and as stiff as she is.'

He nodded his head, and moving one hand from the wheel placed it over hers.

'We're runnin' into the Bay Road,' he announced. 'We'll get cleaned up and line up some grub. I feel kind of empty. We should've stopped for some food on the way.'

He drove the rattling jalopy along the rugged highway and turned off left up towards the line of shacks that stood on a small bill overlooking the wide sweep of the Bay. There was a hotel sign-board creaking and groaning as it swung on its rusty hinges in the breeze.

'This is it,' said Jimmy. 'Guy named Purcell runs it. Used to be a friend of my father's: looks on me like a long-lost son. I'll check us both in an' then I'll have a word with him in private. Meanwhile maybe you could do somethin' about orderin' up some food, huh?'

She smiled sadly up at him.

'Y'know,' he said, simply, 'there's quite a lot of Pat in you.'

'Thanks, Jimmy,' Rita smiled.

Purcell was standing on the wooden veranda of the hotel. His eyes, creased by the sun, opened wide when he saw Jimmy braking outside.

He ran down the rickety steps to greet him, scarcely noticing his companion.

'Jimmy Stratton!' he cried. 'I thought you were . . . say . . . Is this jalopy hot? You shouldn't have.'

'Keep it for now,' Jimmy said, shaking hands. 'You heard about the trouble I'm in?'

'Yeah. The papers were full of it. But you'll be okay here for a while. I wondered if you'd show up. I reckon you had enough sense not to get tailed, huh?'

Jimmy laughed. It was the first time Rita had seen him without the grim, tired look on his face.

'Nope. We weren't tailed,' he said, climbing out of the jalopy. 'This is a friend of mine. No names, Jake. We'll stay as long as it's safe — I don't want to get you into any trouble with the cops. Park the jalopy in the barn. We won't want it anymore for a while. I'll give you the dope as soon as we've cleaned up.'

'Okay. Say, that's a fine-looking dame you've got there, Jimmy. I heard you were gittin' married . . . '

'This isn't Pat,' Jimmy said. 'Just a friend. I'll explain later, like I said. How about some action, Jake? Let's bring that luggage inside.'

He helped Rita out of the car and together they walked into Purcell's tumble-down hotel.

8

Cornell, his usual calm completely destroyed, stormed up and down the room cursing and fouling the air with vituperative epithets directed towards the absent Molari.

'The swine must have doubled back — probably tailed me here. He's picked up the dame. That's the last ruddy straw . . . ' he blustered. The two thugs with him in the room didn't pass any comment. They were two mean yegg-men — the two guys Cornell had brought back to Vallant's flat to clean up. Cornell's best men had gone — shot by Molari's mobsters in the affray which had misfired. Instead of working over the Molari mob, someone had blundered — Mr. Cornell. And Molari and his henchmen had reduced the ranks of the Cornell battalion considerably. Freedsom had died with a chest pitted with .45 bullets. Evans, Todd, Lemming, Kane and Podge — all of them had handed in their chips and turned up their toes. Cornell had been lucky — one accidental slug through the shoulder, a mere scratch.

'We'd better get rid of the stiff,' suggested one of the yegg-men, somewhat fearfully. The night had gone badly and the atmosphere it had left was not a happy one. Neither of the two yegg-men felt at ease. There was something about Cornell at that moment which scared the living daylights out of them, and the knowledge that the Cornell empire was tottering made them worry about their own skins.

Cornell swore harshly.

'Yeah. Take him to the jalopy. Drive him out to the river and dump him. Don't leave any mess. Make a proper job of it. We're in trouble enough as it is.'

The two mobsters bundled the corpse of Vallant into a blanket and carried it hastily out of the room, down to the waiting auto. Cornell was still standing by the bed, swearing under his breath and clenching his flabby hands. The sweat poured from him and all in all he looked a pretty rough sight.

When the two thugs returned he yelled at them:

'We gotta do something about the dame. Molari's got her. Get rid of that stiff and double back here right away. I gotta think.'

Thus dismissed, the men nodded and went about their business, leaving Cornell still yammering away under his breath.

It was a good half hour before they came back, stealthily creeping round the rear of the premises. Cornell was still standing by the bed.

'Well?' he barked.

The spokesman said: 'Okay. We fastened some lead to his feet and threw him over Saddler Bridge. The water's deep enough there.'

'We're all washed up,' growled Cornell savagely. 'That rat's played his ace, I guess. But I ain't finished with him yet. He came back and took the dame. That's settled it. I'm gonna get him.'

'You're askin' for trouble, boss,' muttered Sparkie, scared. 'We're outnumbered some five to one now. Our best trigger-guys are stone cold. We don't stand a chance.'

Cornell scoffed: 'I ain't askin' you to do nothin',' his eyes threw bitter scorn at the two frightened gunmen. 'I don't expect you rats to follow through anymore. I guess you think I'm done for, too, huh? Well, I ain't. *I ain't.* That filthy skunk ain't gonna get away with this. It ain't the dame — it's the damned principle,' he growled, with almost pathetic sincerity. 'An' for that I'm gonna fill Molari so full of holes he'll spray blood like a garden hose . . . '

'You'd better take it easy. Don't do nothin' while you're all burned up, boss. You gotta be reasonable. The guy's all puffed up with what he done. He's on top an' he knows it. He'll be musclin' in everywhere from now on, an' there's nothin' we c'n do about it. We'd do better to lie low for a while. Maybe some of the guys'll feel the same way you do. We gotta have some sort of strength. We lost a lot of guys tonight . . . '

'Aw quit readin' me the late news,'

snapped Cornell. 'Let me think.'

'We ain't gonna hang around here all night are we?' inquired the other gunman.

'I guess not,' Cornell replied, rather more subdued. 'There's nothin' more we c'n do around here.' His pride had taken the biggest fall over the fact that — as he thought — Molari had scooped the girl from under his very nose. The loss of Betty 'Bubbles' Fox didn't mean a thing to Cornell. But the overall effect of the night's fiasco, terminating in the theory that Molari had doubled back to Vallant's apartment and sneaked off with his girl made Cornell so flaming mad that he was practically ready to commit suicide to get even with his opponent. He imagined Molari had done it just to prove to Cornell that he *was* all washed up. That Molari could take anything of Cornell's, as he wished and when he liked, from then on.

The three men turned to the black limousine parked around the rear of the block. Sparkie drove. Cornell suddenly said:

'Say, I guess Molari will have gone back

to his place on the island. He'll have taken the dame there. Maybe it's worth a try.'

'*What's* worth a try?' demanded Sparkie, harshly.

'Having another crack at that yellow-bellied four-flusher,' said Cornell, his eyes narrowing. 'Yeah, it's worth a try.'

'Not to me it ain't,' said Sparkie, gripping the wheel tightly. 'I'm takin' this jalopy straight back to the house an' I'm gettin' me a night's sleep. I guess we done enough for one session.'

'I said we're goin' to the island,' snapped Cornell.

'An' I said,' repeated Sparkie, looking dangerous, 'that we've done enough for tonight. I ain't stickin' my neck' out on these odds, just for the sake of gettin' some dame away from that lug. As far as I'm concerned he can take the dame an' welcome. There's plenty more dames where she came from . . . '

'You'll do as I damned well say,' snorted Cornell, his hand reaching into his deep pocket. Sparkie growled:

'I wouldn't try anythin' like that boss. I

reckon me an' Tiny here have had enough for one night an' we ain't goin' to the island. Don't try an' get rough with us, 'cos you ain't in no fit state to start anythin'.'

Cornell had drawn the revolver from his pocket and was waving it about in the air. Tiny grabbed his arm and struggled with him. Sparkie, driving, shouted: 'Get that rod away from the maniac, Tiny. Crack him one if he won't see sense. I guess he's lost his head.'

The two men were now struggling fiercely in the rear seat of the car. Sparkie watched them through the driving-mirror.

Cornell snorted: 'You two guys'll pay for this.'

'Pipe down,' Sparkie drawled. 'I guess the best thing we c'n do with you is let you take a nice long walk. You need coolin' off.'

He drew the big auto to a stop and got out. Opening the rear door, he grabbed hold of Cornell's lapels and pulled him out. Cornell was so infuriated he was on the verge of tears. His eyes blazed with anger and he began to pummel Sparkie with his fists. Tiny had grabbed the gun from Cornell's hand and was still sitting in the car, swinging the gun around casually. Sparkle hit Cornell on the nose and hooted:

'We're a few miles from your log-cabin, Big-shot,' his voice held considerable menace. 'You'd better start walkin'. The night air might bring you to your senses. I guess you need the exercise anyway.'

'You can't leave me here this time of the mornin',' snarled Cornell. 'I'll have you two lugs fixed for this. You betcha. I'm still givin' the orders around here an' you'd better toe the line or else I'll . . . '

Sparkie interrupted the irate soliloquy with another fierce jab at Cornell's waistcoat-button.

'For Pete's sake quit poundin' your guns, Big-shot,' he commented. 'I've had enough for one night. I feel kinda tired. Now hit the road an' be a good boy. You're all washed up as far as we're concerned, Cornell. You might as well know it.'

Spluttering speechlessly at this unexpected mutiny on the part of his remaining regiment, Cornell was left standing in the road staring after the disappearing light of the limousine. If he'd been in a foul temper previously he was now almost insane with fury. He stood in the road shaking his fists and swearing hoarsely at Molari and everyone else.

Then he realized that it was early in the morning, a few hours before dawn, and that he had a long, long walk back to his house. Unless he could grab a cab on the city limits.

He controlled himself with an effort and began to walk quickly towards the intersection.

★   ★   ★

The morning papers were full of the gun battle between Cornell and Molari's men. The police department hummed with wild activity. A special assembly of the department chiefs under Captain Scott Ormando decided that the outbreak of gang warfare was not a bad thing in itself: some of the coppers welcomed it. The feeling that it was best for the gangsters to kill themselves off rather than that the city should risk losing the valuable lives of officers in futile attempts to bring the mobs to heel, was widespread.

Cornell had spent a rough night. His lieutenant who always remained at the house to keep an eye on things — Blink Denver — fixed the wound as best he could, and Cornell refused to see Doc Jason, the mobster's medico. Cornell had cleaned himself up and shaved. He'd spent most of the night, wide-eyed, staring at the ceiling, smoking and thinking. And he'd reached one or two conclusions.

He knew he was finished. As an emperor, his days were over. It had been a foolish thing to do — on contemplation. He should have stuck to his original plan and not forced Molari's hand. Both gangsters knew the futility of warring among themselves. The coppers had had the last laugh.

Maybe, thought Cornell, Molari might be amenable to discussing more rational methods of running the two outfits. Cornell did not intend that Molari should realize how great the body-blow had been to Cornell's organization. If he could make Molari believe that he still had a few aces up his sleeve and still possessed a fairly strong force of gunmen, the Italian skunk could be talked into some sort of amalgamation. There was no sense in taking the matter to the extreme of fighting Molari to the last breath. Only the cops would benefit from that. Reckoning his remaining assets through the night, Cornell figured that he had lost the best part of his force: there remained only a handful of second-rate thugs few of whom knew how to handle the set-up. Sparkie and Tiny were evidently mutineers. Maybe they'd turn-tail and hitch their wagon to Molari's star. Cornell knew that Molari was welcoming all-comers, after screening them for possible double-dealers.

As for the dame, now that his emotions had watered themselves down a trifle, Cornell was prepared to forget it. Molari could have her . . .

He reached for the telephone and put a call through to Molari's place. The Rushton. It was several minutes before

Molari could be located. His thin, drooling voice answered:

'Hello there, Woolfy. Is a nice morning, yes? How you feel, Big-shot?'

'I'm okay, Molari,' Cornell replied, clenching his teeth. 'I want to talk to you. I guess we were a little hasty about this bust-up. Have you seen the papers this mornin'?'

'Sure I read the news,' grinned Molari. 'Only I don't see no pictures. How many guys you lose, Woolfy?'

'Plenty,' grunted Cornell, taking a firm grip on himself. How he'd have loved to choke the life out of the swine! 'Plenty. More than I c'n spare.'

'Too bad, Woolfy. Too bad.'

'Listen, Molari. I want to talk business with you. What's your reaction to that?'

'Is a ver' strange idea you got there, Woolfy. What kind business you want to talk, eh?'

'Business. Just business. You bin tryin' to horn in on my territory for long enough. We've done nothin' except shoot holes in our best guys. We've both lost plenty of good boys and to run organizations like ours, Molari, guys is indispensable, savvy? I want to discuss a team-up with you. I figure it's time we got together and joined forces instead of tryin' to wreck each other.'

There was a moment's silence. Cornell could hear some low murmuring over the wire and had an idea that Molari was holding his hand over the telephone and saying something to someone near at hand. Then the Italian's voice said:

'I don't get you, Woolfy. I think you're all washed up. You don't got no more pull around town. I'm a the Big-shot now; isn't that so?'

'If that's what you're thinkin', Molari, you want to get wise to yourself,' bluffed Cornell. 'I've still got more pull in this burgh than you'll ever have, an' it don't do you no good to go around figurin' that you can have it all your own way. If you ain't prepared to talk turkey, just say so, an' you'll find out that Woolf Cornell ain't all that easy to defeat. I've still got an organization and I'm still in business. I got all the contacts out of town, an' I can build up to the same size I was before in no time at all. If you want to go on like this, takin' a crack at me, that's okay. How long d'you figure we'll both last at that rate? There's enough business around here for the two of us. Why don't you see sense?'

Molari sniggered: 'All a sudden you get friendly, Woolfy. It natch'rally makes me suspicious. Maybe I misunderstand you, eh? Maybe we oughta talk this thing over properly, eh? Like you say. Okay, Woolfy. You come round my place sometime an' we discuss the terms.'

'Nothin' doin',' snapped Cornell, pleased with the success of having at least incurred Molari's interest. 'If there's any talkin' to be done, you c'n come an' see *me*. You know where my headquarters are. An' any time you want to pay me a visit, I'll have the guys tipped off so's they don't plug any of your team.'

'That's ver' nice of you,' declared Molari, silkily. 'But Molari, he don't pay no visits. If anyone wants see Molari, he comes to Molari. *Si!*'

Cornell hedged. He knew he'd have to give way. The dice were loaded in Molari's favor.

'Okay. It makes no difference. Sooner than give the cops the satisfaction of watchin' us tear each other's outfits apart, I'll play it your way. I'll come over. Just say when.'

'Any time at all,' invited Molari, generously. 'Always glad to see my friends, eh, Woolfy. I'll expect you anytime at all.'

Cornell grunted. 'Fine,' he said.

'But don't bring all your boys with you, Woolfy,' commented Molari. 'I hate bein' crowded.'

'Okay. I'll be alone,' Cornell affirmed. 'Oh, and say, Molari — I'll make you a present of the dame. You c'n have her.'

'Yes? That's ver' nice of you, Woolfy. But what dame you talk about, eh? Which dame you got on your mind?'

'Quit actin' dumb,' scowled Cornell. 'My song-and-dance spot — you know who I mean. 'Bubbles' Fox. I know you breezed into Vallant's suite last night and hi-jacked her. Well, that's okay. I was through with her anyway. Reckon she was on her way out.'

Molari grinned: 'That's no nice way to

talk about your women, Woolfy. But you made a leetle mistake, Big-shot. I ain't seen your dame — not since I was at the Kitkat for supper a couple of weeks ago. Someone pulls your leg, eh, Woolfy. Someone else walked off with your dame.'

Cornell frowned.

That didn't add up at all. He'd been flaying himself all night with the utter humiliation he felt because he thought Molari had scooped up his woman, and now Molari was politely denying that he'd even seen 'Bubbles'!

Maybe Molari was playing him for a sucker?

Maybe the guy was planning some sort of a trick?

Cornell gritted his teeth.

'Maybe so,' he answered. 'It don't matter either way. Okay then. It's a date. I'll be over to see you. An' watch your boys don't try any funny business, Molari, or you'll be sorry you ever left Chicago.'

The Italian's infuriating snigger was the only reply Cornell received. The line went dead.

Blink Denver, who had listened into the conversation, was looking at Cornell as though the boss was stark-raving goofy.

'You ain't gonna walk inta a trap like that, are you, boss?' he breathed.

'What do you take me for, a green-horn?' snorted Cornell. 'Find that little pearl-handed Lamette pistol that used to belong to Annie. It's in a drawer someplace. It's only a little gat but it's a honey, an' I c'n strap it to my arm where it'll never be found if I'm frisked. I reckon it's gonna come in mighty handy.'

Blink nodded, said: 'You're stickin' your neck out once too often. You don't really figure Molari'd consider a tie-up now? He knows you're all washed up. He knows he can just step in an' take what he wants . . . '

Cornell scowled. 'Yeah? Who says I'm all washed up? It seems to be a common notion around here. But it ain't so. I don't wash up as easy as all that. Now get that rod an' quit strainin' your tonsils.'

Blink went away in search of the deadly little Lamette.

9

Cornell turned up at Molari's headquarters early in the evening. He was taken into Molari's office, a huge, impressive room on the first floor of the Rushton. There were half a dozen other men in the room. The air was thick with smoke. Molari sat serenely at the desk, smiling blandly at his visitor.

Cornell examined his opponent minutely. It was the first time he'd had a real look at him. He was a suave Latin, impeccably dressed. His features were bold and symmetrical, the nose long and full-fleshed. Two bright, black eyes peered out at Cornell from below dark neat eyebrows. The gangster's skin was swarthy and his teeth were like big white stones, evenly set in strong red gums which showed clearly when he smiled. There was a glint of savage ruthlessness in the Italian's expression which the smile did nothing to conceal: it was ingrained in his face like an illustration of his real personality for which the smile was a grim façade.

Molari offered his visitor a cigar and a large bourbon. Cornell sat by the desk, apparently treated as an honored guest.

Molari wasted no time. He talked about Cornell's set-up and answered carefully the questions Cornell put to him about his own developments.

Although both men were tensed and wary, each watching the other shrewdly and coldly, as far as the business discussion went, they were quite open.

Molari agreed that it was foolish to give the cops the benefit of their feud. An amalgamation was actually a good thing. He was all in favor of it. If the terms were right.

If the terms were *right!*

That became the pivot of their discussion.

Molari wanted a half-share in the whole organization irrespective of the financial interest Cornell controlled. In return he was prepared to hand over a half-share in his own financial holdings. It was imperative that the legal side of the business should be cast-iron, because although both gangsters carried on most of their business illegally, they had to have an impregnable front to cover up their invidious deals. On paper, everything had to be legally watertight — for which purpose both gangsters had the services of unscrupulous attorneys.

Cornell tried to hedge, but finally, because he knew that without sufficient men to cope with the organization's various avenues his business would collapse, Cornell gave way. To continue working with a handful of trusted men, against the growing strength of Molari's organization, would have spelt eventual collapse anyway.

Cornell had been frisked before entering the room. He didn't like the idea of Molari having all his bums around him while he played lone-eagle. When he suggested sending for Addison, his attorney, Molari nodded in agreement. Cornell was satisfied that the gangster intended to play along fair and square as far as the business tie-up went.

A telephone call brought a stupefied Addison hastening to the Rushton. Cornell explained briefly that he was to draw up papers of partnership which would be legally watertight. The attorney endeavored to prevent Cornell being hasty, but Molari was insistent that the whole matter be settled there and then.

It took something like an hour before the details were finally settled, and the drafts of the agreements mutually agreed. Then Addison and Molari's crooked lawyer went into conference in an adjoining room, leaving Cornell with Molari and two of Molari's mobsters.

Cornell started to get quite pleasant. The only thing that troubled him now was the fact that Molari had insisted on full details concerning the dope and drug trafficking which Cornell had carried on, unwillingly, because of the first deal in the commodity which had been arranged over his head. He tried to convince Molari that it was a dangerous traffic — being a Federal offence. Molari, however, was keen to take it over as a partner and to extend activities in that field. The profits were exceptionally good. Cornell shrugged. It was Molari's head as well as his own. If he thought he could tackle the proposition, all well and good.

Molari said: 'We've talked plenty. Now we get a leetle relaxation, huh? You come up to my apartment. I want you to meet Bella. You like dames, eh? Maybe you like Bella. We see.'

He led Cornell upstairs. On the third floor a complete luxury suite had been installed, the building having been specially altered to accommodate the large, airy rooms of which the penthouse consisted.

In the living room Cornell stood examining the luxurious appointments which Molari had lavished upon the room. He was astounded to find such an imposing set-up and it gave him a new appreciation of Molari's worth.

Then he saw Bella.

She sat on a divan, curled up, reading.

Molari bent down and kissed her on the forehead and grinning broadly introduced Cornell.

'Bella, you meet good friend of mine. Woolf Cornell. He's a Big-shot in this burgh. Like your little Toni was in Chicago.'

Cornell stared fascinated at the woman on the divan.

She was about twenty-five or so. Her exotic, dark beauty was unbelievable. Her perfect features, glossy, black hair and alluring smile mesmerized him.

She was wearing just a kimono over her undergarments, and the gown itself was carelessly open. Cornell's eyes rested for a moment on the milky white throat, then the girl stood up and shook his hand.

She was of medium height. The opened kimono revealed her shapely figure to perfection. Her hands were small and white, with long, slender fingers, red-nailed.

Cornell smiled back at her. Molari watched him closely.

Then he said: 'You want drink, Woolfy?'

'Yeah. I could use a drink,' nodded Cornell.

Molari brought him a drink. It was good liquor. As good as any Cornell hoarded.

Molari said: 'Sit down. Woolfy, on the telephone earlier you made me a present of — your dame. It was a joke, I guess eh? I don't see your dame no place. Anyway, I don't play the same joke. I, Molari, also have good taste in women, eh? You like my Bella? She's ver' lovely, eh? An' ver' passionate.' He smiled faintly. 'I make you a present of Bella, Woolfy. How you like that?'

Cornell grinned uneasily. There was something here he didn't understand.

'You don't have to rub it in if I made a mistake, Molari. I guess I got the wrong tip-off that's all. I ain't bothered about it. Just forget it. You don't have to make corny cracks . . . '

'Please, Mister Cornell!' sniggered Molari. 'You think I'm joking? Molari doesn't joke. I got plenty other dames. This one is for you. Is a seal to the bargain, eh? Our business deal, eh? You take Bella. She ver' nice girl. Now I must go and see about my affairs. I leave you with Bella. She's all yours. You like that, eh, Woolfy?'

Cornell looked across the room,

161

following Molari's receding figure in puzzlement. The gangster paused at the door. He smiled very suggestively and remarked:

'You have a good time, Woolfy. Bella is goin' no place. She stay here with you. She's all yours. I see you later. Tonight — later. We have some more drinks together an' talk some more business, yes?'

He left the room, closing the door after him. Cornell sat for a moment in complete perplexity. Then he noticed the girl watching him.

She spoke for the first time: 'Don't take any notice of that greasy lout,' she said. 'He thinks every girl in the world is his for the askin'. Sometimes he gets me so sored up I could scratch his eyeballs out. Get me a drink, mister.'

Cornell stood up. He went over to the table and mixed her another drink. She swigged it down without batting an eyelid, which considering the liquor was fairly potent quite impressed Cornell. She was a hard one all right. One brought up in the toughest school on earth.

She said: 'Don't sit over there. I ain't got no disease. Come an' squat by me here on the divan. It's good to have someone to talk to. That lout don't give me much of a time. He's got too many floosies on his agenda.'

Cornell obediently moved himself over to the divan. As he sat down, somewhat awkwardly because he was out of his depth, the woman moved closer to him and snuggled against his shoulder.

'I heard about you, Cornell,' she said. 'Reckon Molari must've been mighty scared of you at one time. You were always a thorn in his side.'

'Yeah?' muttered Cornell.

'Yeah,' she nodded. 'Say, you don't seem very easy, big boy. Somethin' on your mind?'

'Nothin' particular,' he answered. 'Only I don't much like the idea of sittin' here with Molari's dame. I reckon it's not goin' to do me a heap of good.'

'How come?' she demanded.

'I might get *ideas*,' he said. 'An' Molari might not like the ideas I get.'

'Oh,' she said. Then she burst into a

163

wild laugh that echoed through the big room.

She stood up, and moving over to the windows, carefully drew the curtains. The room was bathed now only in the faint light of the lamp standards. She switched the radio on, faint. Then returning to the divan she said:

'Molari wasn't kiddin' to you. He meant what he said. It's maybe his idea of hospitality. I don't mean all that much to Molari, Woolfy. When he said he was transferin' me to your team, he meant every word he said . . . ' She paused. 'In a lot of cases I guess I'd be good and sore. But I ain't. There's somethin' about you I like. Maybe it's the thought that you're a Big-shot. I like Big-shots, Woolfy.'

Every word she said seemed to steal up on his innermost feelings. Her soft low voice was like the purring of a kitten. That was it — she was kittenish. Tantalizingly kittenish. Cornell watched her intently. She swaggered back to the divan carelessly.

Cornell knew he wasn't the sort of man who attracted a woman physically. He

164

had never experienced the love, affection or even the admiration of a woman. Those who had who permitted him to possess them had only done so because he was what he was — an influential, dangerous, prosperous gangster. A Bigshot. Someone who could give them jewelry, soft-living, fur-coats and the rest of the gee-gaws which women in that sphere thrived on.

Bella seemed different. Her attitude towards him was friendly. She almost seemed glad of his company. Maybe that was because Molari jealously denied her much freedom, even though he paid her little attention himself. Cornell sat closer to her when she curled up again beside him. His arm went around her waist.

She kissed him. It wasn't reluctantly bestowed. Cornell reciprocated.

She wore a fragrant perfume which reminded Cornell of Annie — his first moll. Annie who had died at the hands of a copper. His memory was vague, but he remembered Annie. He gripped her more tightly in his arms and felt her soft body pressing against him.

He did not see her free arm stray to the floor and her fingers bend under the divan.

He did not see the hand come away, holding the gleaming short-hilted knife.

Maybe, in his unbelievable ecstasy he did not even feel the sharp, plunging blade as it made the deep incision in his back . . .

He gave a sudden groan and his mouth strayed from her lips. His arms became less taut and the pressure of his embrace relaxed. He breathed heavily, and moaned suddenly with acute agony. Then blood oozed between his lips and his whole body shook. She gingerly drew herself from beneath him, throwing his arms from her. He flopped forwards on the divan, the hilt of the dagger sticking up, reflecting the pale amber light of the standard.

He groaned again and murmured: 'You — double-crossing — bitch — I should've . . . '

And that was all.

A convulsive shudder went through his burly frame as he tried to raise himself up, but found his strength ebbing too swiftly from his body. Death gripped him in as fierce an embrace as that in which he had held the lovely Bella so lustfully . . .

★   ★   ★

Bella moved over to the wall and pressed the bell. A moment later Molari, grinning evilly, entered the room. Bella nodded towards the still figure of Cornell, his back now flooded with blood round the blade.

'You made a nice quick job of that, darling,' Molari observed, standing over Cornell, and dropping his arm around Bella's smooth, white shoulders. She stood looking down at her handiwork, expressionless. Molari laughed lightly, and bent to kiss her.

'He didn't cause no trouble at all, eh?'

'I couldn't do it *quick* enough,' she spat out. 'He's the most revolting slug I ever encountered.'

Molari corrected, sweetly: 'He *was*, my sweet. He *was*. Now get some clothes on my Bella. I'll send for the boys, and we get rid of the big porpoise, yes?'

She sauntered into the adjoining room and closed the door. Molari picked up the house telephone.

He said: 'What time is high tide?'

10

Rita came bursting into Jimmy's room with an excited exclamation on her lips. Jimmy stared at her wonderingly.

'Have you seen the papers?' she cried.

'Nope. But I picked up some interestin' news over at Gopper's Saloon this mornin' . . . '

'Look. Read this . . . ' she blurted out.

Jimmy took the paper from her and scanned the paragraph she indicated.

'H'm,' said Jimmy.

'So they got him after all,' cried Rita. 'You don't know how glad I am to read that! When I think of what that filthy brute did to me that night at Vallant's apartment . . . '

The paragraph gave a short account of the discovery of Cornell's body, washed ashore at Jinnerton's Wharf that morning. A wound of some depth, caused by a sharp weapon, indicated that he had been stabbed in the back and later thrown into the river. He had died of his wound, not drowning.

'Molari, I suppose?' Rita said.

'Could be,' nodded Jimmy, wonderingly. 'But it's a new idea if so. I mean using a sticker. I guess Cornell would be pretty burned up to know that he went out that way. I guess he always figured that he'd go to the happy hunting ground with a belly full of hot slugs — not knifed in the back. It looks like someone else's work to me. Maybe even a woman.'

'You're right there,' Rita assented, savagely. 'I'd have welcomed the job. An' you c'n bet he'll be pretty burned up anyway, the place he's gone to.'

Jimmy grinned.

He looked at Rita. The couple of days they'd spent at the hotel had done the girl a lot of good. She no longer looked worn out and haggard, the bruises and scratches had vanished.

He said: 'Well, that makes it tougher still on me.'

'How come?' she demanded, lighting two cigarettes.

Jimmy sat on the edge of the bed,

dangling his slippered feet over the floor. He replied:

'With Cornell's mob all wiped out and Cornell himself out of the picture, I'm gonna have a hell of a time tryin' to locate the evidence I need to implicate that mob in my spot of trouble. I'll be on the run for the rest of my life.'

Rita sat down beside him.

'You're wrong,' she said. 'Altogether wrong. As a matter of fact I thought so as soon as I read about them finding Cornell's body. We know that Molari's mob shot up most of the Cornell outfit. We can guess that Molari disposed of Cornell — even if someone else did the job for him. One of his molls probably — or some girl in the outfit who got tired of bein' pawed about by the fat slug. Anyway, don't you see what it means? Molari will take over — lock, stock and barrel. He's probably done so. I can guess what's behind all this.'

Jimmy said: 'So what? What if Molari does take over? We figured long ago that something like that was on the cards. But it don't make the position any clearer.

Molari's mob was also responsible for Pat's death — someone belonging to that outfit worked that machine-gun over on the occupants of Beamish's green sedan. But knowing that, doesn't make it any easier to pin down the guy responsible. An' the fact that Molari has muscled in and taken over Cornell's outfit and his entire organization — that don't help either.'

'But it does, in some ways,' she protested. 'Don't you see? I c'n go back. Back to my job. Molari will be in control there now, an' I guess I c'n soon get back into the line. He'll have to like it that way — I got a contract for the Kitkat.'

'Yeah? So what?'

'So this. I'll be on the inside. On the inside of Molari's organization. I'll be able to get close to things. I know that Molari's thugs were responsible for Pat's death. I'll find out which one. I'll get the guy, if it's the last thing I do. And while I'm working on that job, I c'n also find out what I can, about the dope-trafficking. Molari is no fool. He'll have his claws on that side of the business too.

Once we know just exactly how Cornell arranged the shipping of the stuff, we'll have something to work on. We could tip off the cops.'

Jimmy was silent, considering her outburst for several seconds.

Then he said, awkwardly, 'Listen, Rita, you're a swell kid. I guess I know how you feel about Pat — I feel the same myself. But I don't want to see you take the same road. I don't want to see you get into any trouble. Maybe if I c'n get clear of this country I could make a fresh start someplace — somewhere where a record don't mean anything. If I could get away . . . right away . . . It'd be best. Don't you see that tryin' to put one over on this new mob will be too dangerous? They're unified now — their only enemy is the cop. There's no gang warfare any more. The odds are doubled against anyone tryin' to fight these thugs . . . '

'Just what are you getting at?' asked Rita, frowning.

'Only this, Rita. I think we ought to give it a rest. I ain't sayin' this because of myself — I'm thinkin' about you. You're a swell kid. I like you plenty. These few days we've known each other I guess I've come to regard you the same way I did Pat. I admire you for what you started out to do. But I don't want you to get hurt . . . I don't want you to go the same way Pat went, Rita . . . '

She looked at him curiously.

'Say, you ain't fallen for my charms, have you, Jimmy?'

He didn't answer for a moment. Then he said, deliberately: 'Maybe it sounds screwy, but I have.'

She put her hand on his sleeve.

'Y'know,' she said. 'This ain't much of a time to say it, an' I'm still wound up about Pat . . . but it's funny, Jimmy. I feel the same way about you. I never knew I'd get feelings like this for any guy, Jimmy. But I liked you the first time I saw you — the mornin' after you — after you took me away from — from Vallant's apartment.'

He put his arms around her.

'You looked in such a state,' he said. 'I felt so sorry for you. Maybe it was more than that, even. I guess I liked the look of you.'

She kissed him.

'Let's get away from here, honey,' he pleaded. 'Purcell can fix it. We could light out for Argentina or Mexico an' start afresh. The cops'd never grab me. We'd be safe. We could . . . '

She shook her head.

'I couldn't do it, Jimmy. I've just got to see this thing through. Someone's got to pay for Pat's death. If the cops can't do something to stop these filthy rats from terrorizin' the country, then someone else's got to do it . . . '

'Honey, be reasonable. You can't do much against the organized graft and vice that grips this burgh. It's plain suicide even to interfere.'

'Then I'll commit suicide.' she said.

'I guess you mean it, too, Rita,' he sighed, shaking his head. 'But that don't help us any. We've got each other. That gives us something to live for. We're too young to die just yet. Okay — so even if I have to take what's comin' to me from the law, it'd only tie me up for five years or less. Then I'd be free. I want to be free, honey. More than ever now. I guess I want to be with you, Rita. Always.'

He took her in his arms and kissed her firmly, holding her closely against him. 'See it my way, honey,' he said. 'We can't do much good against that outfit now. Let's grab what chance we've got and play our luck.'

She returned his embrace and clung to him tightly. But her voice was determined when she said:

'I'm goin' through with what I started, Jimmy. Then we can talk about other things — if we still want to. An' I'm goin' back to the Club. Right away. I'm goin' to see that lug Molari an' find out how my contract stands. Maybe I c'n get that Italian in a corner and squeeze the truth out of him. An' if I c'n pick up any leads that'll help you get the evidence you want, I'll do that too.'

He seemed dejected with her decision. He pulled her against him and kissed her fiercely on the forehead and eyes and lips:

'You ain't gonna go back there right

away, are you, kid?'

'I've got to do it, Jimmy. You don't understand. It's like something burnin' away inside me. I've just got to get some satisfaction out of that swinish mob.'

'I don't like to see you takin' the chance, Rita,' he protested.

'I know,' she murmured. He saw she was crying.

'Jimmy,' she whispered. 'I'm leavin' here tonight. I'm goin' to the Club. I'll take my chance. But I've got a feelin' it might not pan out the way I — the way I want it to. I've got a feelin' — a dreadful feelin' — Maybe it's got to be that way. I know what I'm doin' an' I'll take the chance. But I love you, Jimmy. I want you to know that. I've loved you every minute of the time we've been together.'

He stroked her soft hair.

'Love me, Jimmy,' she whispered. 'Love me.'

11

Rita went back to the Kitkat Club as planned. The fact that the organization was now controlled by Toni Molari meant that an entirely new method of management was in force and Molari, with ideas of his own, had already instituted some drastic changes.

A number of the former members of the staff, including the strong-arm men and bouncers left over after the fight between Cornell's outfit and Molari's, remained. But Molari had added some new people to the Club, and had also carried out some alterations to the rear of the premises, extending the space devoted to the gambling tables. With Cornell's entire organization in his pocket he felt pretty pleased with himself. Even Cornell's private suite had dropped into his lap, and therein he had installed the luscious tigress Bella Miller.

Molari's acquaintanceship with Rita

had been slight up till that time. He had seen her and spoken to her, but casually and with little display of interest. Now that she had returned to the Club to resume her berth as the star of the cabaret, Molari immediately exhibited a greater interest.

For one thing, he was getting a little tired of Bella.

Molari liked changes. He was constantly altering things around, making structural changes in his premises, refurnishing his headquarters, redecorating his offices and constantly investigating new avenues for the dissipation of his energies. He was tireless, restless, unsettled, like a frustrated man chasing something intangible and never able to get his paws on it. And he was a ruthless, sadistic man, with neither conscience nor feeling.

The night Rita returned to the Club, she did so quite casually, as though she had never been away. She consulted only the band-leader — who remained with his outfit — and arranged with him for her two spots that night.

Molari had installed a man named

Harris as his new manager. Nick Harris had formerly been a bootlegger and was *au fait* with the routine organization of a joint like the Kitkat. If he thought anything at all about the fact that 'Bubbles' Fox had shown up again and was performing as usual, his thoughts were strictly sensuous.

She observed the effect she was having upon Harris with acute satisfaction: it solved for her the problem of making a lot of excuses for her recent absence. Harris learned that she had been Cornell's girl, and telling himself in strictest confidence that his own boss, Molari, was tied up pretty firmly with the gorgeous Bella, he considered it highly probable that 'Bubbles' Fox would be easy meat for his own attentions. Molari might harbor strong desires, figured Harris in the back of his machinating brain, but Bella Miller was not a woman to be trifled with or double-crossed. There was little chance of 'Bubbles' putting Bella's nose out of joint where Molari was concerned. Harris even believed that Molari was scared of Bella.

For a few days things went along fairly

evenly. Molari was preoccupied with the consolidation of his enterprises. Harris was equally busy getting to grips with the running of the Kitkat, and several outside jobs which came under his aegis — anything connected with liquor was his work. Molari was an efficient organizer, and the strength of the outfit was now considerable, his own mob linked to the remnants of Cornell's brigade. His lieutenants screened every member of Cornell's outfit, and except for two whose loyalties towards Molari were questionable, were added to the growing Molari payroll. The two uncertainties vanished from human ken with surprising swiftness, and a couple of days later their riddled bodies were taken from a lonely barn out in the country and transferred to the morgue to await identification.

Rita read the reports in the papers about the slaying of the two former Cornell mobsters. One thing struck her as important regarding the police investigations. The rifling on the bullets extracted from the two corpses was identical with that on the slugs taken from the bodies of

Pete Beamish, Guppy the Grid and the unidentified girl — Pat — whom Cornell's mob had known as 'Honey' Delmar.

At last, Rita realized, she had something concrete to work on. It was evident that Molari had ordered the dispatch of the two men. It was not positive that he had executed them himself. But the weapon employed was the same one that had slain the three occupants of the sedan on the island highway. And someone, somewhere inside the Molari outfit, possessed that weapon. A castrated machine-gun of some sort.

After her show on the night after the finding of the two corpses, Rita was called to the telephone in the foyer. It was Jimmy. He was calling from a drug-store somewhere on the edge of the city.

'I can't talk too much here, honey. I had to contact you despite what you said. I'm on the lam again. Some cops came nosin' around Purcell's place and I had to beat it out the back. It's no good, Rita — I've got to get away. I can't be hounded like this.' His voice was low and hoarse. 'I'm waitin' here for Si Lung — he's bringin' me some clothes an' things. Now listen carefully: Si Lung's got a pal who runs a boat for the Acme Shipping Line. It's due to leave Perridale tomorrow night at high tide, from Dock 14. I'm goin' aboard as a Chinese deck-hand. The boat calls at Panama. I can jump the ship there and make for Mexico. It's my only chance of freedom. Are you listenin'?'

Huskily she said: 'Yeah. I'm listenin'. Go on.'

'I'll get in touch with you somehow from Mexico. I know a guy there at San Angel. As soon as I'm fixed okay I want you to join me. You'll do that, honey, won't you?'

She was sobbing a little.

'Do you have to go?' she said.

'I've got to go,' he said, positively. 'It's a chance I might not get again, kid, surely you see that? I'm sick of bein' trailed and hounded like this. Every minute I expect some cop to jump out at me and stick a rod in my guts. Rita — I'm relyin' on you. I want to know that you'll follow on. As soon as I send you an address. Promise me, darlin'.'

'I can't promise anythin',' she whispered. 'I can't, Jimmy. You know that. I've got to get this thing straight first. Can't I see you somewhere before you go? We can't talk over the 'phone.'

'No. There's no time. I've got to hide out until the boat clears tomorrow.'

'But Jimmy . . .'

'Hell,' he grunted suddenly. 'There's someone comin' into the store. Looks like a hoofer. I'll have to beat it. Take care of yourself, honey. I'll be in touch with you. G'bye, Rita. I've got to make a run for it . . .'

The line went dead.

She stood for several seconds looking dumbly at the receiver, her eyes misted over. Then she shook herself out of the mood, replaced the receiver and quitted the box. Harris was hovering around by the main entrance to the Club. He moved over to her.

'Bad news, honey?' he asked, trying to seem concerned.

'No. No,' breathed Rita, gripping

184

herself. 'Just a — just a message.'

'I thought for a moment you'd had some kinda shock,' he said, easily. 'I'm glad it ain't nothin'. That was a swell show you put on tonight, kid.'

'Thanks,' she muttered, walking away.

Harris followed her.

He was right on her heels as she entered the dressing room. She said: 'I've got to get changed. Beat it.'

He entered the room behind her and closed the door.

'I been watchin' for you a long time, sweetheart,' he said. 'Don't give me the brush-off. You an' me oughta get to know each other better.'

'I guess I know you well enough,' she answered. 'You're just the same pattern. Now let me get dressed.'

'Don't mind me,' he grinned. 'You c'n get changed. I want to talk to you.'

'What about?'

'How about comin' out for a bite to eat,' he suggested. 'I know a nice little joint over the river . . . '

'No thanks,' she said. 'I'm tired. I need to get my beauty sleep.'

'You don't need no beauty sleep,' he drawled. 'Quit actin' hard to get.' He moved nearer to her. His arms circled her waist.

'Don't be a fool, Harris,' she cried. 'Molari'll kill you for this.'

He laughed. 'Molari nothin',' he growled. 'You was Cornell's dame, wasn't you? Well, now you c'n be mine. I c'n do a lot for you kid. Why don't you be sensible? Gimme a little kiss.'

She pushed him away and backed towards the dressing table. Picking up one of the candlesticks she raised it in the air and threatened him:

'Clear out of here, you lug, or I'll spoil your looks.'

His eyes glinted. He moved forward. She threw the stick but missed his face, for which she aimed. The stick struck him heavily on the right shoulder. He grinned, but without amusement in his expression. She became frightened.

'I like a dame with spirit,' he said, advancing. His arms again gripped her, tightly. She was surprised at his strength. She could feel his face coming nearer, his mouth searching for her lips. She struggled fiercely, fearing to call out or scream in case he became violent. Her fingernails dug into his neck and her knee flung up and caught him a painful jab in the groin. He swore harshly, and gripped her more tightly.

His hot breath made her feel sick.

Molari walked in at that moment.

His faint tap upon the door was the only signal to Harris, who had overlooked the importance of locking the door.

Rita had a glimpse of Molari's face — the acute expression of astonished disbelief at what he saw. Then she watched him move, like a flash of lightning, towards them. His hands caught Harris by the neck. He turned the flabbergasted manager round and gripped him by the lapels.

Then Molari's right hand drew back, the fist closed, and he lashed out with tremendous force, punching the manager clean on the jaw.

Rita heard the snap as the bone gave. Harris didn't cry out — he merely gurgled, and then collapsed in a heap in the corner of the room, sliding down the wall with his back.

Molari pulled his sleeve down over his cuff again and straightened his necktie. His eyes were roaming over 'Bubbles' as she stood trembling, shivering, her teeth chattering together, one arm extended to the dressing-table to steady herself. Molari kept his gaze centered on her. He was still as calm and unmoved as he'd been when he'd struck Harris. Only his eyes betrayed what he was thinking. The expression increased as he scrutinized her. She could feel his eyes boring into her flesh, but for the moment she was too winded and too upset to care.

Then he said: 'I'm sorry that happened, 'Bubbles.' I'll deal with Harris when he comes to.' He threw her a wrap from the back of the door. 'Don't catch cold, honey. You look ver' upset. You need a leetle drink, eh?'

He pulled a flask out of his hip pocket and handed it to her. She drew the wrap around her aching body and eagerly took the flask. It contained brandy, and she poured it down her throat gratefully.

Then he said: 'You know some'ting? Cornell, he once told me he give you to me for a present. Ha! A ver' generous hombre, was Cornell, eh? He think at the time I had taken you from him. Is a mistake, no? But now I don't know. You're ver' nice 'Bubbles.' I like you plenty.'

She watched him like a cat watching its prey. There was an insolence about his whole demeanor which intrigued her. He was so calm, so cool, so cocksure of himself. He went on: 'Maybe I take Cornell up on the deal, eh? How you like to be Molari's special friend, eh?'

Rita drew in a sharp breath. She tried to keep her voice controlled. Molari was her enemy — the man responsible for Pat's death. She'd waited a long time to put her plan into final operation. Now it looked as though she might at last have a chance to even the score.

'I guess little Bella wouldn't like that, Mr. Molari,' she commented.

Molari chuckled.

'Bella. She's a ver' nice dame, yes. Molari likes the best of every'ting. But

Bella, she's not any trouble. No, Bella she not cause no trouble. You get dressed, honey. We go to my place, eh? We have a drink, an' we talk, eh? You feel better after your leetle shock with Harris. I come back in fifteen minutes. You be ready, eh? That's a good girl . . . '

He smiled broadly at her, flashing those big, white teeth. She nodded, silently, returning his smile.

He went out. At the door he turned and said:

'I'll send one of my boys to get Mr. Harris outa here, eh?'

She nodded again.

★ ★ ★

Molari drove himself, in the big cream sport coupé he reserved for his own pleasure. Rita lay back against the upholstery, her lips tight together, stealing side glances at him, planning things, thinking things, building up her hatreds.

She realized they were driving over the island. She knew Molari had a secret hide-out there, and guessed they were

190

heading for that place. The gangster evidently promised himself a nice, cosy *tête-à-tête* with a new plaything.

They drove up to the dark building, Molari running the automobile straight into a wide garage whose doors opened and closed automatically.

He helped her out of the vehicle, and led her up a flight of steps leading straight from the garage into a spacious hall. As he closed the door behind them, Rita took a quick glance around. The wide paneled hall was like that of some solid old mansion. He beckoned her through to the larger of the rooms leading off from the hall: a rectangular, tall-ceilinged living-room, spacious and airy, delightfully decorated and appointed. The very luxury of it took her breath away.

He grinned:

'You like the place, eh? I spend lot of good money on this place. I like the best.'

He took her wrap from her and indicated a low, comfortable-looking settee, sited by the broad hearth in which a bright log-fire roared. Evidently Molari had been expected, and Rita figured there must be someone on the premises attending to the details of the welcome.

He mixed some drinks and sat beside her.

His voice drooled on, telling her a lot of remarkable reminiscences which included some of his experiences as a top-ranking mobster in Chicago. He made no attempt to paw her or even touch her. He seemed content for the moment to sit, staring into the fire, smoking, drinking and talking. She began to feel drowsy. Her mind, constantly working away on schemes to even up her score with him. She had to play carefully: Molari, as she well knew, was no fool. The slightest hint on her part that she was a danger to him, and her life would be worth less than a chipped nickel. To combat the drowsiness stealing over her she concentrated on his talk and threw in occasional conversational prompters.

An hour after they had arrived, there was a slight buzzing noise on the desk behind them. Turning round, as Molari himself turned, Rita saw a light flickering on and off over the house-'phone box on the big mahogany desk.

Molari frowned and stood up. Moving across the room he flicked a switch on the panel and said:

'Yes. What's the trouble? I told you I don't want to be disturbed . . . '

A voice said, gruffly: 'It's Baines, chief. I had to follow after you. Spike told me you'd left for the island.'

'Well, what's the matter?'

'Trouble, boss,' said the voice. 'The cops identified that gun. The one we used on those two Cornell rats.'

'I know that, you fool,' snapped Molari. 'It's in all the papers.'

'Yeah, but they also picked up some dabs off one of the buttons on one of the jerk's coats. I must have handled the guy rough, an' left a dab on him. On a flamin' button! Can you beat that?' growled the voice.

'You dumb fool!' said Molari, rubbing his chin. 'You'd better skip town. They got your record. They pick you up plenty fast. I don't want no trouble with the cops. Maybe they know you're one of my boys. Come up here. I want to talk to you.'

He flipped the switch back again and stood for a moment scowling down at the desk. Then he walked back to the settee and picked up his drink from the table and swallowed it in one gulp.

He started to talk again to Rita. Explaining to her what a bunch of fools he had to keep his eye on. That Baines — the guy who'd just signaled — for instance. Baines had had the pleasant duty of killing two of the Cornell boys who hadn't wanted to toe the line under Molari's stewardship. Molari had decided they'd have to be disposed of. Baines had been detailed for the job. Baines was a good trigger-guy, but a dumb fool.

After filling the two guys with slugs, he and another Molari mobster had hidden the two bodies in a barn to delay discovery. It had been low-tide, and there was too much danger in dropping them into the river. In handling them Baines must have left a bit of a print on one of the coat buttons of one of the dead guys. The police department was scientifically smart — they'd taken smudges of the dab and now they could easily trace the killer. Baines had a record. One slight error had put the whole gang in jeopardy — because it would be easy to link Baines with Molari. And the worst part of it was that the gun Baines had used was the same weapon with which he'd killed Pete Beamish, and Guppy the Grid and some unknown dame . . . And the cops were mighty concerned about the death of that dame because they thought she was maybe just an innocent kid Beamish had picked up on the road. A hitcher — just an innocent pick-up . . .

He told Rita all this, his eyes narrowed, the muscles of his jaws working away as though he was chewing something at the back of his mouth.

'Baines is a fool. A careless fool . . . ' he said, slowly. 'We'll have to do something about this . . . '

But Rita was no longer listening.

She'd heard enough.

She knew now who had been responsible for the death of Pat. One of Molari's thugs — the guy named Baines.

The guy who had slipped up on the newest dual slaying, and thereby left himself wide open for a murder rap. Her whole body trembled.

Baines!

And he was there — on the premises. On his way up to the room in which she sat with Molari!

Molari was as much to blame as Baines, she said to herself. He'd only acted on Molari's orders. But Baines' was the hand that had pulled the trigger and sent the stream of hot lead pouring into poor Pat's soft flesh. She took a grip on herself. Had to keep calm. Mustn't let Molari know the truth about her . . . about her innermost burning hatred for him and his mob . . . for Baines.

There was a sound outside the door. Molari stiffened. Someone entered. Rita didn't want to look at him. Didn't want to stare into the face which had so cold bloodedly sighted the target for his bullets . . . The man who had deliberately and callously slain Pat . . . He walked towards Molari.

'I could use a drink.' he said, hoarsely.
Molari grunted.

'Help yourself, Baines. On the table.'

The thug poured himself a straight bourbon.

'You were a fool to come here, Baines,' Molari said, coldly. 'The cops might be tailin' you.'

'Yeah. I know,' said Baines. He was an ugly, big-built, unkempt man, with large ears and thick lips.

Rita felt sickened by his very presence. Her wits were straining to think of some way of exacting retribution. But she hesitated. She had a feeling that all was not well. Molari was acting peculiarly.

'What you gonna do?' quizzed Molari.

'Get outa town, of course. But I need some dough. Some moulah. I thought maybe you'd have some dough here. I'll need a lot. I gotta keep in hidin' till the heat's off.'

'Ah, so you want some dough, eh?'

'Yeah. You must keep some around here, chief. You owe me plenty as it is. Gimme ten grand and I'll get on my way. I don't want to hang around here. But I gotta have some dough.'

'Sure. Sure,' said Molari, softly. 'You gotta have some money. That's only right.'

Rita tensed herself.

Molari was staring at Baines.

'I'll get you some dough an' then you'd better get on your way, Baines. The cops might come around lookin' for you, eh? I keep some dough in the safe in the other room. You wait here, I fetch you some money. Help yourself to another drink, Baines.'

He walked across to the door leading to the adjoining room. Baines watched him go, and then swiftly turned to Rita and pulled out a gun.

He motioned to her to keep quiet, the threat in his eyes only too obvious. Then he walked towards the curtains screening the door leading to Molari's private room. The gun in his hand was held firmly, steadily.

Rita took a guess at his intentions. Having learned that Molari kept money in the other room, the thug, knowing that he had to quit town and take it on the lam, was evidently proposing to force Molari to empty his safe into Baines's pocket. Baines probably knew there was a whole heap more than ten thousand dollars in that safe, and he wanted as much as he could get — the lot if possible.

Rita could sense his intentions, but she could also sense something else. She knew, positively knew, that Molari had not gone into that other room with any intention whatsoever of bringing dollars out to Baines.

She waited apprehensively

Suddenly the curtains waved aside and Molari came back. He pretended to be surprised to find Baines standing in front of the curtains, threatening him with the revolver.

'What's this, Baines?' he demanded, icily.

'Since I gotta blow,' said Baines, 'I might as well collect whatever you got in that deposit box, Molari. I'm on the run an' I gotta rap or two comin' to me if I'm caught. Another killin' ain't gonna bother me none. So open up and unload,

Big-shot. I'm takin' all you got in that there tin box.'

Molari scowled.

'You're gonna regret this, Baines,' he snarled.

Baines jerked the gun forward.

'I ain't got much time,' he warned. 'I oughta be leavin'. Let's see some action, Molari. Get back inside that room an' open up that safe again . . . '

Then came the shot.

It was fired from the opening in the room-paneling at the other side of the room. Molari just stood, silently, as Baines dropped to the floor with a grunt, a bullet clean between his shoulder blades.

'It's a good job I don't take no chances, eh, 'Bubbles',' he grinned at Rita. Then turning to the opening in the wall-paneling he said to the two eyes, which were visible through the dark aperture, 'Sharpe. Get this lug out of here, pronto. Get the jalopy out an' take him to the highway. Dump him in the ditch. Then drive out to the Club an' bring some of the boys back here.'

A moment later a little man entered the room. Molari had stooped and retrieved Baines' gun and thrown it on to the table alongside the soda siphon. The newcomer, showing surprising strength for a small man, bent down and bodily hoisted Baines in his arms. Rita watched him, fascinated, as he limped out of the room again, without a sound.

Then her eyes caught the glint of the revolver by the siphon. Molari was closing the door after the man and his cargo . . .

Her mind swiftly pondered her next move.

Baines was dead. The man who had fingered the gun that had slain her sister was now as lifeless as Pat. For that much she was gratified. But Molari was not going to escape unscathed for his part in the tragedy. Baines had acted on Molari's orders. It may be true that Pat had not been elected to be killed: but that was beside the point. The death of Molari was as important to Rita as the death of Baines had been. She remembered Molari's instruction to the little man about bringing some of the mob back with him after disposing of Baines' body. For the moment, assuming that the man had been the only other occupant of the building, she was alone with the gangster. Strangely enough the thought didn't scare her.

He was looking at her, wondering what her thoughts were. No doubt the expression on her face betrayed some of her feelings. She pulled herself together. Molari sat down beside her and for the first time made a movement towards her. His arm went around her shoulders and he said:

'I'm sorry. I guess this little trouble cause you some upset. I'm sorry, 'Bubbles'. Now it is all over, we can relax for a time, eh? Sharpe not come back for some time. We are alone. No one to trouble us, yes. Molari doesn't show you much attention, eh? Now it will be different. Now Molari make love to you eh?'

He kissed her gently.

She controlled herself with an effort. She wanted to keep his mind off that revolver lying on the table within reach of her hand. She must lull him into a state of unwariness, and then make the plunge . . . her hand could grab that gun, point it into his guts and fire it before he would know what had happened. She had to get him into a state of comparative security . . . His hands were fumbling . . . she didn't resist. She kept telling herself it wouldn't be for long . . . it would soon be over . . . His hot, wet lips scoured her face. The Latin blood was roused at last. She felt his weight against her, his hands growing warm and clammy . . . He started to kiss her chin and neck, bringing his insatiable mouth down towards her throat . . . His eyes were closed and his breathing now more uneven. Slowly she loosened her arm and let it drift towards the table, the fingers extended towards the revolver . . .

Her fingers touched the cold metal of the gun. Slowly she drew it towards her, her free hand stroking the back of Molari's neck, to impress him with her surrender . . .

Then she directed the barrel and held the gun an inch from his back . . . and exerting all her remaining strength pulled the trigger with her thumb.

The blinding flash and terrific report seemed like the explosion of a landmine to her. For a moment she was hysterical, a low sob vibrating her whole body. His hands relaxed, and his body seemed to jerk convulsively. He tried to say something, but no words would come. He made one futile attempt to grip her throat . . . Intuitively she knew that if he could have reached her slender white neck, he would have throttled her with his last dying energy . . .

He died painfully, blood streaming from his mouth. She tried to push him off her, but finally had to drag herself from under him, leaving him lying in a frightful posture, face sunk into the cushions. The gun had slipped to the floor . . . She left it lying there . . . Frightened now, and trembling all over . . . she grabbed a glass and shakily poured herself a drink. The brandy flushed her mouth, fired her throat and made her gasp. Droplets of it trickled down her chin.

She looked down at her clothes: the

dress was torn and her brassiere broken. She snatched up the wrap from the chair and drew it around her, feeling chilled to the marrow. Her inside felt sick and revolting. Her mind was in turmoil: she remembered the powerful little man, Sharpe. He'd be returning shortly with some of the Molari thugs.

Rushing from the room she looked for the door in the hall which led to the garage. The car was still there — Molari's big roadster. Sighing with relief she started the engine. Then she remembered that the gates opened automatically and realized that the weight of the car over part of the garage floor would fling the doors apart. She drove forward. The doors slid up, permitting a burst of crisp, fresh, night air to flow into the garage.

She drove out into the night, gulping in the restorative air, deep into her lungs.

She took the road she remembered vaguely, and there were big tears in her eyes as she eventually drove onto the main highway leading across the promontory to the mainland. It was dark and cool. The sky above was filled with heavy, forbidding clouds. She felt cold and lonely. But her heart was considerably lighter, and with every mile taking her closer to the city lights she felt more composed and more relaxed.

Then she wondered what she should do next.

She could not go back to the Club, and she dare not go to her apartment. The car, too, would have to be left somewhere. Molari's thugs, as well as the police, would soon be on her tail.

She drove into town, using the side-streets as much as possible. Then, suddenly, she knew what she must do. A name struck a chord in her memory — the name of Si Lung Fi, the Chinaman.

She turned the car around and headed for Chinatown.

12

The chugging of the tugs on the river: the sirens occasionally blasting the silence of the night. The lapping of the waters against the quay. Overhead the sky filled with a million twinkling stars. The air fresh and crisp, laden with the strange mixture of dockside smells.

The two hurrying figures, courting the shadows, keeping close against the warehouse.

The gang-plank, rickety and barnacled.

Rita walked along it unsteadily, grasping the rough rails with her slim fingers. Behind her shuffled the dark, shrouded figure of Si Lung.

At the top of the gangway a stout man barred their path.

Si Lung pushed his way in front of Rita and said something in low tones to the man. His words were unintelligible to Rita, but evidently he spoke Chinese. The man drew aside and let them board the boat. Then he led them along the deck towards the bridge.

The Chinaman stopped at the steel ladder and called out a few sibilant words.

The man who came down the ladder was scruffy-looking and bearded, wearing an oily, stained uniform and a peaked cap. He greeted Si Lung warmly. From under the folds of his loose clothes the Chinaman drew out a package. This was handed to the captain whom stowed it immediately inside his tunic.

'This the girl?' he enquired.

'Yes. Velly nice lady. You give her good tlip, please. Make Si Lung velly happy.'

'The guy's below. I didn't tell him nothin'.'

'Si Lung velly pleased to know Mr. Lazaritz cally out instructions implicity,' intoned the strange Chinaman.

'Okay. We leave in five minutes,' announced the captain, eyeing Rita intensely in the dim light from the oil-lamp under the bridge-housing.

'I say goodbye, pleasant tlip, missee,' said the Chinaman, turning to Rita.

'Jimmy Velly good boy. You take good care Jimmy, yes?'

'You betcha, Mr. Lung Fi,' said Rita, softly. 'An' thanks for your help. I'll never forget it.'

'Goodbye, missee,' he said, and shuffled off into the darkness. She watched his frail figure vanishing into the gloom of the dock. Then she turned to the captain and said:

'Take me to — to — his cabin.'

'Aye, aye, miss,' said the captain.

★ ★ ★

Jimmy looked up.

His mouth dropped open, letting the cigarette slip from between his lips. He jumped to his feet and moved forward as she closed the cabin door.

'Rita, honey! Rita! How did you get here?'

'I'll tell you. There's *plenty* to tell you! But all I want to do just now is get a breather. I've been through hell since yesterday . . . '

He threw his arms around her and

drew her close, kissing her ardently on the lips and eyes.

'Gee, kid, I was never so pleased to see anyone in my life. I thought maybe I'd never see you again . . . '

She kissed him. His hand closed tightly over her own.

'Molari's dead,' she told him. 'I shot him. An' the guy who killed Pat — he's dead, too. Molari had him shot. He bungled a job . . . '

They stood locked in one another's arms for several moments, in silence, holding on to each other. The boat moved away from the dock: the water lapped fiercely against the sides. The vibration of the engines shook the little cabin. Out in the river sirens screamed.

In a few rapid sentences she told Jimmy about the experiences of the previous night.

She started crying softly.

He pulled out a handkerchief and wiped her face.

'There ain't nothin' to cry about, honey. We're free. In a few days we'll be in Mexico. We c'n make a fresh start. Gee

— it hardly seems real. I guess it's a dream . . . '

'It's no dream,' she said, half smiling, half crying.

He took off her coat and flung it across the chair beside the bunk. His eyes ranged over her admiringly. Her thin, silky dress contrasted deeply with the drab environment of the cabin. She returned his gaze, evenly, amused by his expression.

'We're together now,' he murmured. 'For keeps. The past is dead.'

'Yeah, dead, Jimmy. The past is dead . . . ' Then: 'The skipper of this barge is okay, I suppose?' she asked.

'Sure he is,' grinned Jimmy. 'Si Lung's got him just where he wants him.'

'That's great!'

She moved closer to him, putting her arms around his shoulders. He stroked her silky hair, pulling her against him and kissing her gently on the lips.

'Jimmy, tell me you love me, again,' she whispered.

The boat rocked gently.

He picked her up and carried her to the bunk.

The boat tossed and pitched heavily, rattling loose objects on the walls. Water sprayed against the port-hole. Slowly the boat edged out into the ocean. The engines were steady now, the vibrations even. Somewhere outside there were noises of ropes squealing through pulleys. Then the noise of the ship's bell.

Locked together in the intimate confines of the cabin the two lovers on the bunk were oblivious to all noise, all activity . . . Their thoughts had hastened on ahead to Panama, to Mexico, to a new life, free from the violence and brutal horror of the past.

As dawn broke in the heavens, they stirred.

'Pat would be glad. I know she would,' whispered Rita.

THE END

We do hope that you have enjoyed reading this large print book.

Did you know that all of our titles are available for purchase?

We publish a wide range of high quality large print books including:
Romances, Mysteries, Classics
General Fiction
Non Fiction and Westerns

Special interest titles available in large print are:
The Little Oxford Dictionary
Music Book, Song Book
Hymn Book, Service Book

Also available from us courtesy of Oxford University Press:
Young Readers' Dictionary
(large print edition)
Young Readers' Thesaurus
(large print edition)

For further information or a free brochure, please contact us at:
Ulverscroft Large Print Books Ltd.,
The Green, Bradgate Road, Anstey,
Leicester, LE7 7FU, England.
Tel: (00 44) **0116 236 4325**
Fax: (00 44) **0116 234 0205**

To Chief Inspector Sharkey, the first murder is baffling enough: on a night-club dance floor, a man suddenly begins to choke. Horrified onlookers watch as he collapses and dies. It is quickly established that he has been strangled by someone standing directly behind him. But witnesses all testify that there was no one near him to do it. When this death is followed by a whole string of similar murders, Sharkey begins to seriously wonder if Scotland Yard is up against something supernatural . . .

THE JOCKEY

Gerald Verner

A man calling himself the Jockey begins a campaign against those who he believes have besmirched the good name of horse racing, escaping conviction through lack of evidence. In a message to the press, he vows that those who have amassed crooked fortunes will have the money taken from them, whilst those who have caused loss of life will find their own lives forfeit . . . When the murders begin, Superintendent Budd of Scotland Yard is charged to find and stop the mysterious avenger. But is the Jockey the actual murderer?

MURDER AT ST. MARK'S

Norman Firth

Dr. Wignall, Headmaster of the venerable public school of St. Mark's, is fiercely proud of the institution. But this pride has been considerably shaken by the murder of a teacher's daughter in the nearby woods. As Mr. Prenderby, the charismatic master of North House, uncovers a sordid undercurrent of gambling, blackmail and immorality amongst the schoolboys, another murder is committed — this time, one of the pupils. When one of the teachers bolts, the police think they are trailing the killer — but are they?

THE BISHOP'S PALACE

V. J. Banis

Elizabeth Parker comes to Brazil to take up a job as a schoolteacher in the declining city of Manalos, skirting the Amazonian jungle. Hoping to start a new life, she instead finds forbidden love with the husband of her employer, the aristocratic Kitty Drayton, who lives in a decaying mansion with her spinster sister. The atmosphere of unease surrounding Elizabeth steadily grows into terror as she is stalked by a sinister figure during Rio's Carnival, culminating in a shocking murder — for which she becomes the obvious suspect . . .

THE SILVER HORSESHOE

Gerald Verner

John Arbinger receives an anonymous note — offering 'protection' from criminal gangs in exchange for £5,000 — with the impression of a tiny silver horseshoe in the bottom right-hand corner. Ignoring the author's warning about going to the police, Arbinger seeks the help of Superintendent Budd of Scotland Yard. But Budd is too late to save Arbinger from the deadly consequences of his actions, and soon the activities of the Silver Horseshoe threaten the public at large — as well as the lives of Budd and his stalwart companions . . .